POLITICALLY INCORRECT BIBLE STORIES

Dear Rachel!
Anticipating a glorious time together.
Rachel

POLITICALLY INCORRECT BIBLE STORIES
Is Sex Good for the Jews?

Rachel Patron

iUniverse.com, Inc.
San Jose New York Lincoln Shanghai

Politically Incorrect Bible Stories
Is Sex Good for the Jews?

All Rights Reserved © 2000 by Rachel Patron

No part of this book may be reproduced or transmitted in any form or by any means, graphic, electronic, or mechanical, including photocopying, recording, taping, or by any information storage retrieval system, without the permission in writing from the publisher.

Published by iUniverse.com, Inc.

For information address:
iUniverse.com, Inc.
5220 S 16th, Ste. 200
Lincoln, NE 68512
www.iuniverse.com

This book is a work of fiction. Names, characters, places and incidents are products of the author's imagination or are used fictitiously. Any resemblance to actual events or locales or persons, living or dead, is entirely coincidental.

ISBN: 0-595-15899-4

Printed in the United States of America

In memory of my ancestors
36 uninterrupted generations of rabbis
And especially my grandfather
Rabbi Jacob Meyer Rakowski

Acknowledgements

To my husband and children, who rarely consider me funny.

Many thanks to the staff of the Prosser Public Library in Bloomfield, Connecticut, who allow me to blend into the woodwork.

Deep gratitude to my agent, Professor James Schiavone, for his help and encouragement.

Last, but not least, thank You Lord for giving us the Bible.

Foreword

Is Sex good for the Jews?—is not a frivolous question, and the answer to it far from obvious. For all the other peoples of the earth it may be a resounding YES; but for the Jews? Well, the matter requires more—and deeper—exploration.

Why have I been Chosen to conduct this inquiry? You see, recently I've written the poignant story of my fascinating life—my grandmother was couturiere to the courts of two great Polish kings, Little Lech White and Little Lech Black; my eccentric and amorous relatives cavorted all over Europe in pursuit of enlightenment and pleasure; I spent two years in an orphanage without a dog called Sandy...—only to be told "Too Jewish," by the mostly-Jewish editors.

Clearly, I must write something that'll sell, I told myself. But what? At that fateful moment I remembered my late mother's sage advice: Ripped Bodice!

Right on! Mom must be referring to Sex!

I reached for my trusted yellow pad and wrote on it with my No. 2 pencil: S-E-X. (I'm an old fashioned girl and write everything in longhand first, which may explain why my life is so uninteresting to the Silicon Valley generation.) For a while I sat there, contemplating this exciting, one-syllable noun. Sex! Problem is, what does one do with it? Delving into my female core I asked myself: What is the subject about which I know the most? (Never mind how much I don't know about sex!) One word sprang to mind: JEWS.

I wrote it down next to Sex.

Now I have two nouns in close proximity: SEX and JEWS? What's the connection between them? Nothing comes to mind. Hmm, this time let's think like my Dad, his memory be blessed. For example: when I called him on that fateful Friday in November, 1963, when President John F. Kennedy was assassinated, he asked: "Was it a Jew?"

"Of course not," I said. "Lee Harvey Oswald is not a Jewish name."

"Don't be so confident," he responded, with a centuries-old fatalism, "before you can say Knickerbrocker, a Jewish name will be involved in this." Ah, the infallibility of Jewish fathers! Apparently, what lurked behind my father's ridiculous question was my people's ages-old anxiety: Is this—or that, or whatever—good for the Jews? Yes, this is where my contorted thinking is headed: If I combine the two nouns—Sex and Jews—I shall reach the question which has confounded mankind since times immemorial: IS SEX GOOD FOR THE JEWS?

And where do you find the largest number of Jews doing things to each other over the longest period of time? Why, the Bible, of course! The Good Book should clarify, God willing, just how good sex has been for the Jews throughout the ages.

I am also uniquely qualified to conduct a biblical inquiry by virtue of my pedigree: My mother's family tree is traced back to Rashi, the most famous Jewish scholar in 11th century France, who, in turn, is a direct descendant of King David, the-once-and-future Messaiah. Naturally, since my fore-forefather David, Son of Jesse of Bethlehem, was a great contributor to the successful interaction between Jews and sex, I, his offspring, am uniquely qualified to conduct this research.

Allow me a general observation on the moral-sexual premise of the Bible: SEX IS FINITE! Read the Bible carefully and you'll see that Jews have pioneered the concept that there is only so much sex to go around in the universe, i.e. an individually pre-determined SEX

QUOTA. In other words, the earliest Affirmative Action On Sex known to humankind. The rationale for it is simple: Everyone is entitled to such and such a ration of sex. No more! If you get more than your fair share—I get less and I'm not going to take it! We have all seen that if one guy, be he the mightiest of rulers, gets too much sex, the Council of Elders will pounce all over his extremities.

More on this anon.

Finally: It is my sincere intention to devote myself to sex alone—unless it proves insufficient to sell this book; in which case I shall resort to some exhilirating and gruesome violence.

Amen!

1

The Creation Story
or: Who's on First?
(Dedicated To The Non-Simian Dwellers Of Kansas)

Genesis, Chapter 1

I'm the Fly on the Wall, known in Hebrew as Zebub, not to be confused with Baalzebub, a revolting gentile insect. I, of course, have not yet been created, and neither has the Wall, but as literature demands, you must suspend disbelief. So where's the sex? you may ask. It's everywhere, stupid! Creation without sex is like Veal Florentine without spinach.

Let me assure you at the outset that God has always intended to possess Heaven and Earth. The difficulty was that he couldn't find them. In vain did He travel far and wide in the atmospheric nothingness of those days. Heaven and Earth were nowhere to be found. Angry as hell, you should pardon the expression, He produced the Big Bang. Chaos ensued, a really God-awful mess. You couldn't tell vapor from plasma, let alone Heaven from Earth. It was only at this point that I Fly whispered in God's ear: Order must come from Chaos!

God replied with a meaningful: Aha! And immediately launched Himself into creating stuff: First, the aforementioned Heaven and Earth, then various bodies of water, such as oceans, rivers, and puddles on the kitchen floor. The profusion of liquids was followed by grass and fruit trees, so people could water their lawns, relax in the shade of their trees and stuff themselves with bananas.

But nourishment of the stomach is not enough to sustain life, so God created the Love Song. In no time lovers rhymed pretty words into verses, but they were prevented from doing things to each other by the prevailing darkness. What we need is the light of the silvery moon, cajoled a representative of the Moon Lobby, eyeing a young couple frantically groping in the dark. On the Third Day God obliged, and contracted acid reflux from listening to the endless pairing of Moon and June.

The Leviathan was a mistake. The Lord never intended to create a fish that big, even if He'd known how much inspiration this mountain of blubber would provide to the practitioners of ancient philosophies. Truth is, not being a deep thinker Himself, God doesn't give a hoot about philosophy. He emotes. He feels your pain. Here's what really went down regarding the monster fish: On the day He was slapping together halibut, swordfish, and filet of sole out of a mountain of solid blubber, He felt an overpowering urge to visit the Outhouse in the Sky, leaving the blubber unattended. When He came back relieved and eager to resume Creation—the mass was gone, floated away like the Titanic. Conclusion: the Leviathan was also a disaster.

The incident convinced God to pay more attention to fish size. The result was the carp, the pollock, and the lowly smelt. But what was done, could no longer be undone. The mammoth Leviathan lurked in the depths, eating up dolphins and flounders as fast as God created them, and aspirating the smelts in through his nostrils.

Everyone worried what the Leviathan would eat when the fish ran out. God's answer: SEX. Let me make one thing perfectly clear: Sex was not conceived as people-pleasure, but as Leviathan-food! As The Good Book says: Be fruitful and multiply because The Fish is hungry!

As the sixth day dawned, God created ME, the insecure flying gnat, surrounded by all manner of beast on the ground, and winged creatures, such as birds and bees, in the air. Very pretty, I thought. But the Almighty was not satisfied.

"Is this all? Is there nothing more to eternity?" He asked, sweeping a nonchalant hand over what He had created. "I need something je ne sais quoi, something truly beautiful. A sight so ravishing that it'll satisfy my yearnings, my urges, elevate me to Divine Rapture…"

In this state of ecstasy God created Woman. "Bingo!" He cried. "I got it on the first try! She's all I've ever dreamed of!"

God provided Woman with a fine piece of real estate known as the Garden of Eden, replete with an imaginative assortment of fruit trees and a soda fountain to refresh herself. In the beginning her name was Evelyn, but after the Leviathan fiasco God shortened it to Eve, preferring one-syllable names.

God said, "Eve, of all the pretty fruit in this garden you're forbidden to eat only one, the Apple."

Eve addressed the Lord with barely hidden disdain: "If I'm not supposed to eat from the apple tree, why did You create it?"

"No reason, I suppose…But if you don't make an exclusion, how can you enforce a rule? Well said, ha?'"

"Whatever," Eve replied, yawning prettily.

She was a total BB—Bored Beauty. In the Garden of Eden nothing changes: The same sweet pomegranates, bonsai shrubs, gorgeous flowers. She couldn't amuse herself with Horticulture because God fancied himself a gardener. Time to drop the attitude, Eve decided, and sweetly asked, "My dear Lord, how can You call this the Garden of Eden? A maiden can die of lassitude."

"Lassitude? A fancy word. I haven't created it yet."

"Sorry. There's a lot you haven't created. Yet!"

"What's that supposed to mean?"

"Why should I have less pleasure than the smelt?"

"How so?"

"'Be fruitful and multiply!' You say this to a sardine! How about me, Lord? How about me?"

"How about you, what?"

"How about my sex life?"

"Ha, ha, ha! You can't do it without a mate! And I happen to be God."

"Right."

"Oh, I see. But I created you for myself and have no intention of sharing!"

"Yes, yes, I understand, my sweet Lord. But You are not anatomically correct, and thus not capable of fulfilling a lady's needs."

"Oh, shit, you don't mean the gross anatomy?"

"Ha, ha!"

God asked with resignation, "What kind of man would you like me to create?"

Eve had to slap her cheeks to stifle her mounting excitement. "Well..." she drawled. "I...I need someone earthy, a rough and tumble sort of guy."

God was fuming with righteous indignation. "How about character? Integrity? Nobility?"

Eve shrugged her pretty, bare shoulders. "Oh, a couple of functioning parts are more essential."

"All right!" He raged. "I'll give you a no-frills Man, all stripped down. With the body of a Mac truck and the brain of a pinhead!"

"Right, Lord," Eve grinned contentedly.

The Lord cast a deep slumber on Eve, and when she was under, plucked some DNA from her big left toe and created Man, whom He called Adam at first, and never cared enough to amend it.

When Eve came to she happily remarked: "Even with an aching toe I'm mighty thrilled to have gotten me a fella."

So delighted was the Lady Eve with her new toy that she played with it day and night. Indelicately put, her exuberance for sex was at such a fever pitch that she wouldn't allow the poor new specimen to relax or throw on a grass loincloth. Eve was the happiest woman alive.

She was the only woman alive.

But Adam was dragging. Man, oh, man, was he getting a workout! All God intended to do was supply Eve with "a helpmate," an Auxiliary Force, so to speak. But Eve was abusing the privilege, not even allowing Adam free time for a snack and turning him into a gaunt and bedraggled Thing. But how could he say NO, after she sacrificed a toenail to acquire him. There's a moral dilemma for you, Doctor Laura!

Which brings us to the snake, not one of my favorite reptiles. You see, at first Moi the Fly intended to attract Adam's attention. I hissed in his direction, cocquettishly flapping my tiny wings. No response. Clearly, size does matter. Realizing the futility of my endeavors I asked the snake to be my stand-in. When that sliding, sniveling, smoothie hisses—creatures in the wild listen. His French name is Ennui, Boredom, a language that hasn't yet been invented, because in Eden we use cuneiform, a language that hasn't yet been spoken. In any event, by now the haggard Adam was ready for a wily French seducer.

Snake's opening gambit was mellifluous. "Oh, Adam, I can plainly see that something is bothering you. What is it, old sport?"

Adam shed a hot tear. "I'm nothing but a sex slave. That's all she can think of, SEX! It's on her mind morning, noon and night. I have turned from a toenail to a sex object!"

"Yes, Adam," the snake agreed. "You deserve better. What would you like her to do?"

"Just for once I would like to be appreciated for my soul, my intellect. I'm Adam The Body, but I want to be Adam The Brain."

"I can fix it for you easily."

"How?"

"Eat an apple from yonder tree."

"Yonder tree is verboten," Adam informed.

"Aren't you curious why?"

"Ha?"

"Where's your sense of discovery, sport? Your spirit of adventure?"

"Had you been as worked over by Eve as I am, you'd have little taste left for adventure."

"Oh, c'mon, man! Let me taste the apple for you." The snake licked the apple with his curvaceous tongue. A crunchy bite followed. "Yummy, best apple I've ever tasted. And watch! Nothing evil is happening to me. I'm still a snake."

The snake exhibited such delight in the apple, that Adam could no longer resist. "Let me have a bite!" He grabbed the apple, hungrily biting off a piece. "Delicious! I love the sweet, juicy fruit."

As he glanced down at himself his face registered a puzzled expression. "Would you say that I'm naked?" he asked the snake.

"Nakedness is in the eye of the beholder."

At that moment Eve strolled up to the pair. "What are you two doing? Eating apples behind my back? What's next? Smoking cigarettes?"

The Snake cackled. "Ha, ha, ha."

Eve stretched her arms over her head. "Personally, I'd rather be fruitful and multiply."

Adam groaned in anguish, as Eve grabbed one of his relevant extremities. Suddenly he smiled, shaking his delicious curls. "No multiplying for you, Eve, unless you have a bite of my sweet apple."

"Oh, anything you say." Urgently Eve sank her teeth into the apple.

Thunder, lightening, and His voice from Above. "What have you done, Eve?"

An unfamiliar instinct propelled Adam to place his hands over his crotch.

"Wherefore are you touching yourself, Adam?" roared an angry God.

Adam became as crimson as a Red Delicious. "Methinks I'm naked, Lord."

God uttered a Divine witticism. "You are what you are. I think."

Adam was crying, hot tears falling down his cheeks. Eve was furious at her Maker. "See what you've done with Your lack of finesse. Now he'll be useless to me!"

God appealed to Eve's loftier nature. "Young woman, there's more to life than coitus."

Eve looked down at the snake, and by God—she got it! "It's all his fault!" she shouted. "I'll crush him as the lowly cockroach that he is!"

She tore a branch off the apple tree and smashed it on the ground. But the ground was bare. The wily Frenchman had slithered away.

2

How to Marry off Five Daughters in the Middle of A Flood?

Genesis, Chapter 6

The Good Book would have one believe that God took care of all contingencies before flooding the earth with millions of cubits of water. So allow me, Na'ama Noah, the Missus, to set the record straight. Yes, part of the above statement is true. In His wisdom God took care of everyone, from the ant to the zebra, including my three sons: Shem, Ham and Yaphet…

But not my five girls! My five single, Jewish, available, lasses. How does a mother find eligible bachelors while floating in an Ark on the seven seas?

You must forgive me. I am so agitated. I should do my breathing exercises to stop these palpitations. Thank you, I'm better now. Very well, then, let me start in the beginning, that is, the age known as Before the Flood. The truth is that God didn't plan the flood with paper, pen and a timetable, which are the appropriate actions before such a shindig. On his part, my hapless Noah couldn't plan a breakfast meeting of two Elks. No, whatever good came out of that sordid mess, was my personal achievement.

Lucky for them, because my presence was an afterthought. At first God commanded Noah to send all creatures into the Ark in pairs. When my hubby saw all those four-legged couples marching up the gangplank, he realized that something was wrong with the picture. "Hello, Lord! How about me? What am I supposed to do with myself? Be a third wheel to a couple of amorous sheep?"

"Oh, very well," sayeth the Lord. "Take the old nag, as long as you get on with the boarding."

The name Noah means "Easy to get along with," in other words, a "schmuck," you should pardon the expression; but with water reaching up to my neck, I have trouble finding the most delicate words. My name, Na'ama means "The Pleasing One," in other words, a victim. Believe me, staying married to Noah for five-hundred years goes beyond "pleasing." Of my husband the Good Book says: "He walked with God." When? may I ask. I don't remember ever letting him out of my sight, and I have personally never observed him strolling hand in hand with the Almighty.

Still, I'm willing to drop the issue of credibility and concentrate on the painful problem of marriage It appears that after God paired off everyone, including my boys, He thoughtlessly drowned Yenta the Matchmaker, leaving my five single girls—Alisha, Batya, Catalina, Desdemona, and Ed—marooned and drowning. My babies have less prospects for a good match than the daughters of Tevye the Milkman.

I can't catch my breath, honestly. One, two, three; one, two, three. Easy now. On top of all else I've been claustrophobic since birth. And I can't swim! All my life I've required vast expanses of desert. Sweeping yellow is very soothing, but azure blue gives me angst. My jitters have increased because for the past 40 days and nights I've been stuck on this rickety boat, listening to the laborious copulations of huge farm animals. Would any creature, under like circumstances, remain The Pleasing One?

Between us I'll confess that I've even tried to match up my daughters with a male chimp, a gorilla, a gibbon and other simians approved by Mr. Darwin. But, oh, the shame! The monkeys wouldn't have them! "We have our own beautiful playmates," they'd smirk.

In anguish I cried out to the Lord, "My daughters have been rejected by a baboon!"

"Let them hump a camel," He giggled.

"Lord, I disapprove of vulgarity," I said, outraged.

"Very well, I apologize. I suppose I ought to do something in regard to your...hm...problem." His voice drifted away.

For two days and nights nothing happened...On the third day, in the middle of the stormy sea, 5 brawny guys in skimpy leopard skins landed on the Ark, as if from outer space, and announced that they are the Sons of God on a mission to marry my daughters. A likely story, I thought. These guys look too human and yummy.

On the other hand...it's not as if my girls have a horde of suitors, or are likely to have any in a generation or two, and by that time—I shudder to think—they won't look good to either a baboon or a primitive man. Besides, these boys are Jewish...and what with...

"Very well," I agreed. "It's a match made in heaven."

With my girls off the Ark, I turned back to the misery of the Flood. The way I see it, God's expectations of humans have exceeded His investment in them. He made Woman from a breath of air, and Man from a toenail. Not many raw materials went into this process. So why does He expect us to be virtuous? God, you're all wet, and humanity deserves a second chance!

You're inefficient, as well, sending down the Flood before contracting a shipbuilder for the Ark. Then You come up with the insane notion that my husband, Noah, a peripheral figure in this entire saga, should build You a boat. Scared the shit out of the old guy. As always, I stepped in and hammered the box together. Make a note, world: Women make excellent engineers.

They might also make great Gods, if given half a chance. No, I know the truth: God is a man. A woman would have planned a major operation such as the Flood with more precision. We are detail people, perfectionists.

Anyway, here we are, stuck in the middle of the costliest, most mismanaged undertaking of all time, floating on MY Ark on the seven seas. Perhaps eight. With so much water—who can tell?

It's funny the things you remember when water is up to your armpits. For instance, the bumper stickers we used to pin on donkeys' tails: "I'd rather be sailing." Not so! After what we've been through, give me a burro any day of the week. On them you can be a solitary rider, not a steerage passenger listening to beasts fornicating on God's orders.

My mistake was allowing Noah to navigate my ship, and dearly have we paid for it. Instead of landing in St. Tropez, as the Lord promised at first, Noah shipwrecked us on Mt. Ararat, the most active volcano in Turkey. We were in physical and mental shock for a week. After that everyone, including God, forgot what a fiasco the Flood had been, and treated us to a mighty display of Fire and Light known as "The Rainbow"—another costly, ineffective extravaganza.

I cannot gloss over a final unpleasantness: What do you think my husband does as soon as he steps on dry land? A decent man would go out to gather wood for a fire, kill a deer for supper, find a warm cave to shield his weary family?

Not so Noah! He gets drunk! Yes, sodden, stinking, idiotically-grinning drunk, prancing in the tent in his birthday suit!

If I were God, I would have cast him back into the sea.

3

Sodom and Gomorra
A Sentimental Journey

Genesis, Chapter 18–19

Much has been written about MCS, the Middle Child Syndrome—but nothing about MAS, the Middle Angel Syndrome? Clearly, it's time to shed light on this terrible mental disorder which afflicts one-third of our angel population.

Why does God refuse to dispatch Angels down in pairs? Why always in threes? Perhaps, as I've suspected for a billion years, it's something He's got against me personally, since I am always cast as THE MIDDLE ANGEL. I played this role in The Three Kings; The Three Wise

Men; and The Three Magi. If I were doing Macbeth, I'd be the Witch in the Middle. I won't mention the Holy Trinity for fear of having my feet cast in cement and floated on The Moribund Lake.

Having flunked Existentialism 101 in Angel U, I've been designated as the No-Name-Angel and given less respect than Rodney Dangerfield. The Angel to my right is A; to my left, the no less eloquent B, but I am X, named after a bunch of incoherent files.

My latest tale of woe started, as all of them do, inauspiciously. Our angelic troika's assignment was to inform a 120-year old woman that she would give birth to a son. Why? I have no idea. Suffice it to say that a large part of our missions is in the field of obstetrics.

So here we are, in the tent of this really ancient couple, Abraham and Sarah. When we tell them about the baby, Sarah grabs her bony hips and starts laughing: "Yeah, right! I think you boys are hallucinating from walking in the desert without a water bottle. Look, Aby, their brains have turned into cactus mush." So far, all this discourse is between A, B and the woman. Not until she mentions "cactus mush," does anyone look in my direction.

The old lady's husband, Abraham, is exuberant. Imagine the thrill of a guy who's been trying, unsuccessfully, to make a baby for 120 years—and finally hits a homer! As a reward for the miraculous news, he plies us with ridiculous amounts of lentils and baklava. On top of which—and this is really bizarre—he refuses to let us go.

I mean, he literally clings to us as we leave his tent. As if having drunk once too often from this man's gourd, we owe him a guided tour of the Dead Sea.

Yeah, the Dead Sea is where we're headed, on God's orders, of course. Our new assignment: to determine whether the inhabitants of the twin cities of Sodom and Gomorrah have whimsy. God, it seems, has heard rumors that though lusty, these men posses a flabby humor bone. Our objective will be to entrap them into a comedic situation.

The four of us—including Abraham, our new appendage—materialize atop the mountain overlooking the Dead Sea. We peer intently to check what's going on below. Nothing. Can't make out an elephant from a gnat, because everything is shrouded in a dense fog, a thick, porous, milky substance. I can barely see A or B, let alone Aby.

"Lord," says A. "Please be advised that the atmosphere down under is too thick for us to investigate the presence or absence of anything as petite as whimsy. So, with Your kind permission, we're off to the goat races."

"Not so fast!" bellows the Lord. "If you can't see from here, get thee down into the valley." What's an Angel to do? The Supreme Being hath spoken. On we stumble into the pea soup.

At this point, for no apparent reason, God ignores A and B—let alone me!—and engages in conversation with our newcomer.

"Abraham!" He says. "The folks here are mighty wicked."

"It's the climate, Lord. What can You expect of people who live on the lowest spot on earth?"

A cackle. "Don't question God's ways of allocating real estate."

Abraham is getting tough. "That's a cop-out, Lord. This place is so hot that their only swimming pool is called The Dead Sea!"

"There's a reason for it."

"Aha?"

"I killed every living thing in it."

"That's very whimsical of You, Lord."

Abraham reflects a while, then asks, "Lord, what kind of depravity are we talking about, anyway?"

"The sexual kind."

"Like I said, the heat and humidity makes one horny."

"The Lord does not subscribe to the notion that environment causes crime. We do believe that a person is accountable for his or her actions."

"Her? You mean my Sarah?"

"Oh, drop it, Aby."

"You give in too easily, Lord."

"Only when human lives are at stake. I never compromise on matters of principle. That's why I intend to destroy everyone and everything in this valley."

"Destroy everyone?" Abraham is stunned. Clearly, he is new to "The Lord Is Pissed Off" game. "What if there are 50 righteous men in Sodom? Will You destroy 50 perfectly good people because of the depravity of outside agitators?"

"Wouldn't bother me in the least." The Great One chuckles. Then He amends. "Your point, however, is well taken. I shall not destroy the city if there are 50 righteous people in it."

Abraham clears his throat: "Ahem…How about 45?"

"45 it is."

Surprisingly, the haggling continues. That's what happens when God starts doing business with amateur mortals instead of us professional Angels. We know our business. He says destroy! We pour on the lava!

"Forty...?" Abraham suggests coyly.

"What did you say?" God thunders.

Does Abraham notice? No, he's a dolt of biblical proportions. "Thirty?" he ventures. This donkey trading is becoming amusing. (We don't trade horses in the Land of Canaan, because those are to be found only in Egypt.)

"I'll go along with thirty," rules the Almighty.

"Twenty..." Abraham whispers tentatively. To misuse a metaphor, I'm wondering about the line in the fog?

"Twenty?!" The Lord repeats with pent-up fury.

"T...e...n...?" Abraham's voice is barely audible.

A roar pierces the foggy sky: "Ten! Ten! Ten! Very well, I'll take ten! But let me assure you that Ten is the absolute minimum! Don't subtract from it a limb or an extremity! Not even a tooth, let alone a whole person! Don't reduce this by a dog, a snake, or a fish. If I have to go into single digits—I shall destroy everything on earth, be it walking, crawling, or levitating..."

Reduced to shivers, Abraham quits and vanishes into the fog.

In the blink of an eye, we, the angels, are transported inside the city of Sodom and ushered into the presence of an elderly gent, who introduces himself as Lot, and invites us to have supper and spend the night at his house. So what's this crap about the people of Sodom being wicked, if the first person we meet is such a sweetheart? We consume a hearty meal of grilled ox testicles over marinated bulghur and are anxiously awaiting our nighttime rest. Between Sarah's disdain, Abraham's angst, and God's caginess—we are wiped out.

But no sooner do we lay our heads on the goatskins, as every male in Sodom—from the youngest, callow youth, to the most crotchety oldster—descend on Lot's house with loud, incomprehensible screams. Our host bursts into our room, eyes popping with fear, and shouts, "The men's hearts overflow with evil intent."

"Have they come to rob us?" we ask.

"No," says Lot.

"Murder us?"

"No."

"Set the house on fire?"

"No!"

"What other evil is there?"

"They want to sodomise you."

Deep down I feel sympathy for the attackers as victims of geographic isolation. Understandably they cannot resist the appearance of a new face in town. Or any other part of the human anatomy, for that matter.

Outside, the attackers continue to proclaim their intention of getting "to know" us. My sympathy for them vanishes when I remember that we Angels are immune from hunger, thirst or sleep-deprivation—but not from this "knowing" business! We get sodomized like everyone else!

In an ingenious strategy, Lot offers the townspeople the first thing that pops into his mind: "Take my two daughters, please. You have my permission to do unto them whatever you like!" What a father! I pray to God that the Sodomites take Lot up on his offer.

"Your daughters, man, are no substitute for these lusty mainland hunks!" is the town's unanimous verdict. My heart swells with pride, until the full ramifications of the men's enthusiasm cast a pall on their compliment.

The mob is breaking down the door. God, where are You when Angels' asses are in the sling? In the nick of time—as He's wont to do—God casts a collective blindness on the attackers, preventing them from locating the door. In frustration, they begin "to know" each other. With a sigh of relief I rub my backside against the wall, while God instructs us to explain to Lot that he must get his family out of the city which is about to be destroyed. So much for His promise to Abraham to search for 10 Righteous men! Small wonder that the Jews had so little return on all the stuff the Almighty promised them.

As if reading my mind, God roars: "You've just failed simple math: Lot and the Missus is 2; the spurned offering, i.e. the two damsels, makes 4; and the-sons-in-law is 6. No need to look any further! So sue me!"

Lot's sons-in-law refuse to leave the fleshpots of Sodom.

"To hell with the sons-in-law!" Angel B. shouts to Lot. "Grab the broads and let's get out of here!"

"You forgot to warn them that curiosity kills the cat," I tug at B.'s sleeve.

"No pets allowed!" B. yells. In angelic circles he's known as an imbecile. At last he catches on. "You mean the business with not looking back?" I nod, and B. addresses the small group in an unnecessarily thunderous voice: "Whoever looks back will be subjected to severe reprisals!"

What dumb language! Maybe "severe reprisals" works for politicians, but people with higher intelligence know that it's a turd in mothballs.

Naturally, Mrs. Lot, another genius, does not comprehend the vague phrasing. While running away from the lava, she hears an intriguing sound behind her, turns around—and is transformed into a Pillar of Salt. Why not gypsium, or borax? you may ask. Because God is not about to import raw materials for the sake of one stupid woman. He's using what's at hand: Salt!

How heartbroken is Lot at seeing his wife suddenly immobilized? That's a tough call to make, because all the Bible says is that he licks his wife from her navel to her breasts, smacks his lips, and declares: Salt! With that he grabs his nubile daughters and sprints away from the approaching Volcano.

The count is down to three dysfunctional humans. Wisely, Lot decides to get out of the path of heated ash and drags his daughters into a cave.

I must confess that the following account of events inside the cave is not eyewitness stuff since God barred us Angels from going in. Still, I have it from a reliable source that the story told in the Bible is not 100% kosher.

The Good Book says that the daughters got Lot drunk, then slept with him without his knowledge or active participation. Really?! Will anyone tell me how one ferments wine in a salty cave? After all, it doesn't say that Lot grabbed his wife, daughters and a jug of wine! And how much time have you got to determine what provisions to take, when boiling lava tickles your feet?

What even the most permissive angelic circles contend is that Lot forced himself on his two daughters—inappropriate behavior that God chose to ignore rather than admit that the only male He saved—is a child abuser. Don't forget that Lot was the one who, but a few hours earlier, offered the same two girls to an unruly mob for the purposes of "knowing?"

The abuse continues with the girls' subsequent loss of reputation: When they get pregnant, God punishes them for their father's misdeeds by making the offspring—oh, horror of horrors!—GOYIM! Gentiles! Moabites and Ammonites! Conclusion: Non-Jews are the offsprings of incestuous relationships.

Years later, as the gascious fumes lift from the Valley of Sodom and Gomorrah, sordid evidence of nepotism emerges: Lot, it seems, was Abraham's uncle! It is clear that dear old Aby tricked God into saving his only blood relative outside the distant land of his birth, Ur of the Chaldeans, formerly known as Eden.

What all this amounts to is the survival of the unfittest.

4

Confessions of A Mohel's Apprentice
or:
The Perils of Mass Circumcision

Genesis, Chapter 34

My name is Itzik Son of Peshi, the Sandal Maker. So why am I not in my father's profession? you may ask. Blind ambition, I suppose. You see, my parents aimed for their son to better himself, and at age 16 secured for me the position of a Mohel's Apprentice; which is the Hebrew word for Circumciser, i.e. He That Cuts The Penis.

Today I'm an old man and President Emeritus of the United Mohels' Union. The fact that such a union exists is in itself a tribute to my long and distinguished career as a Mohel who has made ethical cutting his life's mission. The young generation today is unaware of the struggle that we pioneer Mohels had to endure so that all our sons—cutter and cuttee alike—would have a Mohel Bill of Rights, to ensure that both are not thrown off a cliff when too much of the foreskin is cut off by mistake. We have also enacted the provision that a Mohel must limit himself to removing no more than a dozen foreskins in 24 hours.

What is less known is the incident that led me to become the sponsor of this milestone reform. It took place in my youth, during the Unenlightened Age, when I became the apprentice to the Grand Mohel himself, Hotech Ben Hotech. Shortly thereafter, I found myself in the wrong place at the wrong time, and ended up with the circumcision assignment from hell.

In my mind's eye the events are as fresh as if they happened yesterday: It was a sweltering Thursday afternoon during the slow cutting season, when my boss—to whom I shall refer as HBH—decided to take a long weekend off in the cool mountains of Northern Galillee. "In this weather there'll be no clients, bubeleh," he assured me, "not even a single walk-in."

"And what if someone shows up?" I protested. "You know that I've never performed a Bris on my own."

HBH cackled. "Even if this happens—and I am sure it won't—you'll ruin a single pecker. No big deal."

So here I am the next morning, a Friday, alone in the Cutting Room, thinking of HBH enjoying himself in the cool rolling hills. Anticipating a lazy morning and an early closing time, I have already covered up the Cutting Slab with the Ritual Goatskin Cloth. Dancing the hora I reach for HBH's gourd of red wine, the one he imbibes from to fortify himself while cutting. He always says that drinking wine is a Mitsvah because during Passover Seder you are ordered to drink at least four full cups. Now I take a few innocent swallows, while my bare feet tap out the staccato rhythm of the Mohel's Marching Song.

At that moment I look up from the gourd and nearly gag: In front of me is—Lord, please say it's not so!—a customer! Not an infant, but a youngish man of no more than 80 who looks me over slowly from curly hair to tapping toes and asks with caution. "Are you the Mohel?"

"Well, not really," I stammer, terrified.

"So, where is the Mohel?"

"Well, he, you see, sir...."

"Are you a thief?"

"Oh, no, sir, no! I'm Itzik, the Mohel's Apprentice."

"Good enough," the man says with palpable relief. "I am Jacob, Son of Isaac, your namesake." (In Hebrew Itzik is the affectionate name for Isaac.)

A second later the truth hits me with astonishing lucidity: I know of this guy because everyone in Canaan has heard about his 12 ferocious sons, Alpha males with evil tempers and club-like fists. Their names range from Asher to Zebulun, with Reuben and Judah in between; all of them rowdy and cruel. How will they react to the loss of their patriarch's pecker? Time to pray to Yahveh, the One and Only, and even to the stone idols of Canaan. The only consolation is that after all, I've observed HBH on several occasions, so maybe I've learned a few things. Maybe not. Oh, Daddy, how I wish you'd taught me the respectable metier of weaving Biblical sandals!

"I am offering you a career opportunity to rival that of Ruby Keeler," says my customer.

I don't need a career opportunity! I only yearn for a quiet Shabbat.

"What...?" I stammer.

"Trust me. Trust me."

Very bad. Very bad.

He orders me to fetch HBH's tools, (the ones he has just sharpened in Philistine quarries, because we Hebrews are still in the Stone Age), and join him in his fancy litter. Once there, he instructs his servants to serve us grape leaves stuffed with goat cheese, its consistency and saltiness cementing my palate. Still, I'm afraid to ask for water. Instead, I grin at the benevolent patriarch and pray, pray, pray.

Me and the Patriarch reach a mid-size town inhabited by the Canaan tribe of Hivites. Jacob leads me to the Town Square where laid out, in a neat row, are 400—yes, FOUR HUNDRED!—male Hivites, all of them bottomless, grinning, and yelling: "Cut me first! Me! Me! I must be the first!"

I blink. This can't be. I must be dreaming. I try to clear my throat of goat cheese and come up with a plausible excuse to forestall the imminent disaster. But what excuse? Nothing like this has ever been told even in the tallest tales of Mohel Folklore.

I turn to Jacob, my employer-abductor, and stammer: "There are too many of them. I mean, I can't possibly..."

"Better do it, young man, if you know what's good for you." Ha? Where has the kindly old man gone? What's with this sudden desert ferocity? The tree doesn't fall far from the apple, I guess. As if reading my thoughts, he says, "If there are any problems, I shall dispatch my sons to have a chat with you."

No! I'd rather be circumcised again!

I hear a voice from the head of the bottomless men: "Over here, Cutter Boy!" Clearly, a voice used to commanding men on the battlefield. I rush over, and find myself facing a pair of bare bottoms, one old and flabby, the other young and flexing with vitality.

"I am Hamor," says Flabby Bottom, (which in Hebrew means Ass), "and this is my firstborn, Shehem Son of Hamor."

"But why are you doing this, sirs? Why?" I ask them.

Old Bottom laughs boisterously, hitting his son over his bare buttocks. "Because, finally we Hivites have gained the upper hand over these dumb Hebrews. And you know why? Because of our brains!" He touches his genitals, then hurriedly moves his hand to his forehead. "Brains, yes. You see, my son, Shehem had his way with young Dinah, daughter of Jacob and sister of the Big Twelve…"

God, I don't want to be involved with the Mishpocheh, which in Hebrew means La Famiglia!

"Anyway," Old Bottom continues, "my son actually fell in love with the little lady and wants to make an honest woman out of her."

The two laugh uproariously, which makes their anatomy wobble back and forth. When the movement subsides,

Old Bottom returns to the story, "As is the custom, my son and I go to old man Jacob and offer him anything he wants as bride price for Dinah. 'Take our goats,' we say, 'our sheep, our daughters, fair and obedient...' But these fools reject our generous offers. 'No,' they say, 'all we want is your...'"

A paroxysm of laughter prevents the old man from finishing his sentence. Instead, he winks at me and points between his legs. Coughing, he stammers: "'Your foreskins!' Ha, ha, ha! 'After you're circumcised, we'll give YOU our goats, our sheep and our daughters...'"

The remaining 398 Hivites join in the laughter, their privates shaking violently. Oh God, what have I done to deserve THIS?

Young Shehem tugs at his father's loins. "Dad, let's get on with the Bris! The faster we cut, the sooner I shall be reunited with my beloved Dinah."

Is this the opportune time to confess that I have never performed a circumcision? I look towards Jacob, and my heart sinks into my knees: While I was concentrating on the Hivites' bottoms, the Hebrew elder has been joined by his twelve sons, whose beards are exceedingly dirty and whose sharp teeth glow in the noonday sun like Philistine daggers.

What to do? Small wonder that we Hebrews wrote the Bible. Each day God presents us with a fresh moral dilemma.

I decide that the answer to my plight—is flight! My eyes wander to the town's gate, where, to my dismay, I see that two of Jacob's sons have taken up positions as sentries.

Back to cutting, I suppose.

The long and short of it is that I proceed to cut foreskins for the next three days and nights, the first and only Bris Marathon in history! For 72 uninterrupted hours I see nothing but clipped-off foreskins. Sweat is dripping from every crevice in my body. I pity the last 100 guys I cut, because, exhausted, I do them with my eyes closed. Honestly, if I look at another foreskin, I'll gag.

When I'm done, I drop my cutlery onto the cobblestones. To hell with HBH, let the newlyweds consider this a shower gift.

Not looking back, I flee the Hivite town.

After this incident—which has aged me by three Bar Mitsvahs—I become an advocate of new Circumcision Guidelines, enacted a decade later. According to the new provisions a gentile who desires to be circumcised in order to marry a Hebrew girl, must wait a week before the procedure is carried out. Hey, guys, I know that Jewish women are demanding—but this is ridiculous!

Tell your future mother-in-law that to cut your privates is not in her daughter's best interests.

In conclusion I must add that while the poor circumcised Hivites were "writhing in pain," as the Good Book colorfully puts it, Dinah's feckless brothers slaughtered them all, Ass and Son of Ass included.

In the future, the worst abuse of Circumcision Guidelines came from David Son of Jesse. It appears that his date to the wine-pressing bachanalia, Mihal, daughter of King Saul, did not want a corsage made of lillies, but one woven of 100 Philistine foreskins.

"One hundred!" I told the young man indignantly. " No! Do it yourself!"

"Don't mind if I do," he said. And you know what? He did! Liked it so much, in fact, that instead of the requested 100 foreskins, he presented his beloved with a bouquet of 200.

The Hebrews were so impressed that they made him King.

5

Sexual Harassment in the Age of the Pyramids

Genesis, Chapter 39

This common wisdom cannot be overstated: When a Hebrew walks through your door, trouble follows. I should know, I'm Igor the Aswanite. Until Joseph Son of Jacob entered my life, I was happily employed as goy-toy to My Lady Ishtar, wife of Potifar Son of Potifera, Pharaoh's Captain of the Guard.

I was able to satisfy my lady's every exquisite whim, directional or perpendicular. Tirelessly, I may add, sometimes even joyfully, although she was at least 32 years old at the time. Fifteen times a day Ishtar would stroll into my chambers, yelling: "Goy honey! Let's go!" And I did, I did, oh, how eagerly I obliged.

Then, one night an apparition entered the household. Black curly hair streaked with camel shit, body smeared as well, a loincloth made of sheepskin clinging to his withered rump, his fingers clutching a torn security blanket. "This is all that remains of my technicolor coat," he mumbled. I, of course, had no idea what sort of mantle this barefoot primitif was referring to.

The Lord Potifar told Lady Ishtar a cock n'bull story about purchasing the lad—at a deservedly low price, of course!—at the Flea Market for Discounted Slaves. "What a bargain!" my Lord cried. "When we clean him up, we may find a real mentsch underneath."

"Lord, this one's no bargain at any price," I remarked sagely, my lips curving into a smirk. The randy creature stuck a disgusting black tongue out at me.

Once more the Lord Potifar was proven right; I suppose that's why he's the master and I'm a slave. The pitiful scum cleaned up beautifully. As the days and weeks progressed his skin-and-bone frame fleshed out with workouts at the gym and the daily intake of a multi-hormonal drink. His hair acquired a shiny glow, for which the master rewarded him with a silk coat with gold threaded through it. From then on, day and night he caressed the garment, having apparently contracted an obsessive love of textiles.

As all Hebrews, Joseph was a secret accountant and offered to work on the master's ledgers. A few days later the master ran excitedly—and, for us, inconveniently—into Lady Ishtar's chambers, shouting: "He balanced the books! Oh, great God of Ammon, he's a genius! He balanced the books!"

So impressed was he with the Hebrew's accounting prowess that he appointed him Chief of Staff, the quickest promotion in the history of the Bureaucratic Empire of the Nile! Now, please don't misunderstand me, I'm no xenophobe, some of my best friends are xenos, but there's a limit to my endurance! I'm not saying I'm drawing a line in the sand, because any connoisseur of desert topography will tell you that it's as useless as drawing a line on the Red Sea.

Maybe husbands are the last to know, but nothing escapes the goy-toy. Often I've observed the Lady Ishtar trailing the foreigner, dreamy-eyed. Upon seeing me, she would drool: "Isn't he of beautiful form and fair to look upon?"

Does such idiocy deserve an answer?

At this point our account diverges into he said/she said territory. But since I am a dispassionate observer, I would definitely go with what "she said." The truth is that one afternoon Joseph crept into My Lady's chamber, and dived into her bed. She was in it, of course. Not asleep, but distracted by a metaphysical problem. While he caressed her naked body, she meditated about the Divinity of Ra, the Sun God. Only when Joseph sneezed—did she notice his presence. Righteously, she began to scream: "The Hebrew is raping me!"

"All lies! Fabrications!" Joseph proclaimed later at his trial, while shackled to the pillar of the Ras El Amarna Temple. Because of these developments I was in a good enough mood to stop by and listen to him. "She came on to me!" he said in a hoarse whisper. "She said, 'Have your way with me,' and I said, 'No, madam, your husband trusts me with all his worldly goods; which explains why it's beneath my honor to defile his trust and pleasure you…"

Much later my mistress confided in me that she had grabbed Joseph in the wrong spot: instead of seizing his tutti-frutti, she snatched his silk cloak with the gold threads. Big mistake, because everyone knows that the Hebrews prefer shmattes to sex.

Anyhow, during the trial I took the stand to back up my mistress' account, who, of course, possessed the physical evidence: Joseph's coat! This proved beyond the shadow of a doubt his unlawful intrusion into in her bedchamber.

A cuckolded Lord Potifar had Joseph thrown into the dungeon.

Exit Joseph? I wish! But for a Hebrew the dungeon represents not arthritis, but a career opportunity. What will they dream up next? Conducting business in the belly of a fish?

In the dungeon Joseph had a dream in which he was besieged by 400 bare-assed Hivites demanding their foreskins back. Upon awakening he correctly interpreted the dream to mean that his brothers were hiding something from him; perhaps the aforementioned skins.

Literally overnight, Joseph fancies himself a Dream Consultant, and is soon blessed with two very convenient cellmates: Egypt's Chief Vintner and Chief Baker, both convicted of crimes against Pharaoh.

Joseph greets them with a pat on the back and an expansive grin. "If I can be of any help, gentlemen? Need to smuggle in cigarettes? Perchance interpret dreams?"

"What's a dream?" they ask.

"You know, a confusing story that comes to you while you sleep, of which you can make neither head nor tail when you wake up. Never fear, Joseph's here to tell you front from back."

The next morning the Vintner and the Baker wake up in choleric moods. Wouldn't you, if you were forced to trade a palace for a dungeon?

"Any dreams?" Joseph asks eagerly.

"Well, let me see..." starts the Vintner.

"How about this for a dream?" Joseph suggests, "Let's say you're seeing a branch of plump, juicy, luscious..."

"Yes! Yes! I see grapes!" The Vintner brightens considerably.

"The grapes are between three branches..."

"Why three?"

"Shut up, you illiterate Egyptian bureauc-rat! Don't you know that in the Bible everything occurs in threes? Anyway, where was I? Oh, yes: You, the Vintner, are holding Pharaoh's chalice in your hand." The Vintner's smile broadens to encompass the entire Nile Delta. "You squeeze the luscious grapes to make wine for Pharaoh. His Majesty drinks and belches..."

"He belches?!" The Vintner shouts. "That's a good omen. Pharaoh is always happy after he belches!"

"Indeed. The three branches represent three days. Meaning, that in three days you will be sprung from jail, hold up Pharaoh's cup brimming with wine, and forever enjoy your master's happy belching."

The Vintner claps his hands in delight.

"One thing, though," Joseph adds, "when good fortune shines on you, you must come and get me out of this rat-hole, because if you don't I'll reverse my interpretation."

"Done deal," says the Vintner, and they shake on it.

"Me too!" cries the Baker, seeing the happiness that Joseph brought to his pal the Vintner. "I want to have a dream!"

"Good. Close your eyes. What do you see?"

"Bread."

"What else?"

"Baguettes, croissants, brioches, milles feuilles, petits fours…"

"What? Only French stuff?"

"No. I also see pita."

"Pita! Blah! It tastes like seaweed. You don't deserve to live!"

The Baker cries pitifully, and Joseph says, "Oh, stop sniveling! Let me set you straight: You no longer see pattisserie but three loaves of Jewish bread, Challah, which means that in three days Pharaoh's guards will chop off your head and impale it on the city walls like a big round challah."

In three days, what Joseph predicted came to pass. A sage? Hardly. The warden's pet would be more accurate: Joseph had heard from the Overseer that an order arrived from Pharaoh to release the Vintner and execute the Baker.

P.S.: The final joke is on Joseph; though neither he nor I would be present to witness it. You see, Joseph enjoyed great prosperity, being fruitful and multiplying with each day that passed. So much so that after he died, his descendants numbered into the tens of thousands. At that time a Pharaoh ruled over Egypt who despised dreams and dreamers and made slaves out of the entire Hebrew nation.

6

The Forty Years' Misunderstanding
or:
You Can't Part the Sea with A Gun1

EXODUS—THE BOOK

"I'm ready for my close-up, Mr. De Mille!"

Rubbish! Never happened! I, the Great Cecil B.De Mille, would have never employed a minor starlet such as Norma Desmond. I've always had grandiose ambitions, global, monumental…

Convinced that I was destined to create a GIGANTIC production, I sat down and penned a major screenplay called "The Life and Loves of God." Unfortunately, a battle royal erupted between Louis B. Meyer, Samuel Goldwyn, and Jack Warner, as to who would play the lead, and the project was shelved.

Back at the drawing board, I searched for someone as big as God. And BINGO, I had a vision: Moses, that big, horny lug, what a colossal idea! My first choice to play Moses was not Chuck Heston, but Eddie Cantor. That, however, fell through because Eddie was busy with his endocrinologist.

I asked my friends in the Hollywood Elite who would be best to play Moses, and their answer was unequivocal: Anyone but a Jew!

Chuck Heston was not an easy sell. One thing got him particularly upset. "What do you mean a staff? I'm supposed to run around killing Egyptians with a staff? Do you know what's a staff? It's a stick of wood, goddamit!"

"Chuck, Chuck, Chuck, don't worry," I assured him, "it won't be an ordinary stick of wood, but a spectacular, winding knob, gnarled and majestic like Pharaoh's scepter."

"You ever heard of a gun, Cecil Baby? You give Moses a gun and he'll have his way with Egypt—and Mesopotamia, for that matter."

"Chuckie, baby," I cooed to him soothingly, "You can't part the Red Sea with a gun."

My assistants backed me up in a rousing chorus: "With a gun! With a gun! No, you can't part the Sea with a gun!"

So I am reading and rereading the Book of Exodus. A great yarn. But where's the sex? Parting the Red Sea? Parting, ha? Nah, too existential. So what happens when you can't have real sex? You open up the story and invent some, as we say in the business.

On the one hand, then, I have Moses, the Super Jew for all Seasons; and on the other one generic—but gorgeous!—Siren of the Nile. My first choice for Moses' love interest was Doris Day, but since for her sex meant a romp in the hay with Rock Hudson, I switched to that typical Egyptian feline, Ann Baxter. Completing the triangle was Yul Le Bald with a rally bad haircut.

We are ready to roll!

The Good Book says that the Children of Israel were oppressed in Egypt, all day long mixing straw to make bricks for the construction of Pharaoh's pyramids and citadels. We know they did a good job, because the whole shebang is still standing, collecting the tourist dollar. What would Egyptians live on today without the Sphynx and Giza? Clearly, the hard-working Jews had to sacrifice either sex or sleep in their marathon to build the pyramids.

Personally I'd guess that they sacrificed sleep, because Pharaoh wanted them to be fruitful and supply Egypt with new Hebrew slaves to build more pyramids. Rather than have a few well-rested slaves, Pharaoh opted for a multitude of sleepwalking, oversexed Hebrews.

But the Jews yearned to have everything, especially a nap in-between sex. So the Children of Israel cried to the Lord to liberate them from insomnia. God went out to search for a charismatic leader, a dark, tall and handsome hunk who most resembled a Hollywood leading man. Almost immediately He was discouraged: Hebrew men were all dark, some of them handsome—but none tall! What's a God to do? Is it more difficult to find a tall Jew than to draw water out of a rock?

In this fashion, my script proceeded apace. I felt it deep in my gut that this would be the Greatest Story Ever Told, with all the necessary dramatic ingredients: Good Jews, evil goys, a cast of thousands, or at least as many as the shooting budget would allow. Not that I care how many Hebrews REALLY left Egypt; but since I'm the one directing this spectacle—we'll have a cast of thousands and the finest special effects since the Great Flood!

Still, I felt that my Point of View was a little weak. Try as I may, I was unable to put myself into the skin of Moses the Man. As Lee Strassberg would say: The transference thing between Cecil and Moe was lacking.

Then, one morning a thirsty Bedouin shepherd wandered from the Sinai desert into my office in downtown Burbank, and offered to trade a clay jar which he had found in the desert, for a six-pack of coke and ten tubs of Poland Springs water, to quench the thirst of his flock of sheep parked under my windows.

The deal was struck and the goods changed hands.

With trembling fingers I opened the jar, feeling a premonition of significant events. Sure enough, inside was a sheaf of papyrus which contained—oh, miracle of miracles!—a missive from Moses himself entitled: The Recollections of an Egyptian Prince.

Here, then, are the rescued hyroglyphics:

"My name is Moses, Son of Amram, and I have always considered myself an Egyptian first and a Hebrew third. What's second I can't recall. I am putting these recollections down on papyrus to set the record straight about history's most vulgar travelogue: The Exodus. When I'm through writing, I shall bury these papyri in the sand, though at first I meant to float them in a bottle, but, alas, the Red Sea has not been reliable lately.

The sad truth is that nothing is reliable these days, which also explains the personal mess I'm in. Trust me, none of it is of my doing; I'm more sinned against than sinning, a victim of circumstances, a sacrificial lamb of mistaken identity, a goat out of water, a moose out of its habitat...In a nutshell: I can't understand why all this unpleasantness should have befallen me, a fellow who has always attempted to steer clear of the seamier aspects of life?

Let me assure you that I have always been a staunch Egyptian patriot. Why, in my youth I distinguished myself in Pharaoh's northern campaign against the Hyksos, and received a Purple Sphynx from the ruler himself for stopping with my kneecap an arrow headed directly for the center of his genitalia.

In Royal Healer School, my son excelled as captain of the rowing team which won the Annual Barge Race against the Luxor Mercantile Association. In fact, we have always been such a loyal, all-Egyptian family, that, contrary to today's vogue, none of us would buy a camel imported from Mesopotamia, even if it eats only once in a fortnight, whereas Egyptian camels voraciously consume daily sacks of oats.

So why all this anguish, God, why, oh why?

In retrospect, I think, that all the upheaval is due to an excess of freedom and equality that we Egyptians enjoy. Yeah, Lord, too much of a good thing, or, as my zayde would say: the bride is too beautiful. You see, in Egypt, except for the nobles and the priests—everyone is equal. They partake of the fleshpot twice a week, have two camels in their family stall, and enjoy free tickets to the performances of the snake charmers.

But how can you be happy gorging yourself when you know that there's no one out there who goes hungry? After all, an aristocrat is entitled to derive sensual pleasure from the plight of the poor. Conclusion: the Egyptians must find a group to whom they can feel superior and whom they'll be allowed to humiliate. Running around like ants in heat all over the Nile Delta they chanced upon us, the Hebrews, and observed that we lack gods. Yes, with an s, for plural. Gods, meaning those little people made of clay that the Egyptians carry in their laps or strapped to the backsides of their camels. So what if we Hebrews don't do that? In all other respects we are every bit as Egyptian as the most fervent idol worshipper.

In principle we don't object to having a limited idol menagerie to take along on a picnic or a ride on the Love Canal. The problem is that we don't know what He/She/They look like. It is rumored that in the days of Antiquity Joseph knew what You, Lord, look like, but he was too busy with worldly successes and grain buyouts to transmit this knowledge to his sons, Efraim and Menashe. So here we are, as the Good Book says, in the middle of the Diaspora with not a graven image or a painted mask.

We have been idol-poor for several generations, which is why the Egyptians decided to single us out for inferiority status. In the beginning we were naïve, imagining that inferiority meant being called ugly names and insensitive ethnic slurs. The Egyptians, however, were more creative. They enslaved us by throwing us into a pit and ordering us to mix straw and build the fortified cities of Pitom and Raamses.

Oh, no, we begged, give us another chance to carve us some gods. The extension we received was short, a mere 40 days and nights. If by that time, we were warned, we would produce nothing of artistic value, they would merrily slam the yoke around our necks.

As always, my brethren turned to me because I am a leader of the community, a successful businessman, a philanthropist. My specialty is real estate and my success is due to an uncanny ability to match up the right people with the right land. Practically, though, the biggest help in business has been my ability to stutter at the opportune moment. It's a trick that most real estate agents have not caught on to, and smugly believe that I am eloquence-challenged. Ha, ha, ha! Of course I am, I tell them, as a result of having been exposed to an excess of water in infancy. Here's how the stuttering trick works: When a buyer makes me an offer, I pretend to stand there helplessly, trying to form an S or a T. He, of course, thinks that I'm holding out on him and offers me more money. At which point I get really choked up, and he goes even higher...Conclusion: what makes a great salesman is a timely stutter.

Anyhow, I digress. Let's get back to the dolls. As my Hebrew brethren begged me to find them some gods, I harkened to my stuttering habit, attempting to form the syllable NO! They, however, were not prepared to take NO for an answer. So they eagerly jumped on me, covering my cheeks with disgusting, wet kisses. To regain serenity I headed for the desert to pray to the Great Sphynx. Pardon me, Lord, but IT and I have enjoyed a long-standing, amicable relationship. In the past I have outlined before IT some of my most creative sales pitches, and IT has never contradicted me. A good, reliable friend.

Now, more than ever, I needed counsel. "Oh, great, exalted Sphynx," I said, "would you help me acquire some gods? You know, half a dozen, portable, compact, nothing fancy. We're not Egyptian haute bourgeoisie."

The Sphynx lived up to its reputation for reticence. Not a peep out of ITs mouth. Was it possible that the Great Sphynx has powers to inspire me only in financial matters?

Disenchanted, I turned away and strolled into the vastness of the Sinai desert. The sand has always calmed my nerves…flowing yellowness, undulating, hypnotizing…It brings the poet and lover out in me. As I walked, dusk began to fall. So I sat down under a bush and fell asleep.

The next thing I remember, is that my tush feels exceedingly hot. So I jump up in panic to examine my hot seat, and discover that my entire backside is on fire. "Oh, my God!" I scream. "I'll burn to a crisp! My buttocks will become two lovely chauteaubriands." But even in my agitation, I can't help noticing something odd about the flame: Although my derriere burns and feels hot, I experience no pain and my skin is as pink and clear as a baby's. But the overall problem remains: How long can a successful Egyptian businessman run around Cairo with his ass on fire?

At this precise moment I hear The Big Voice, Yours to be sure: "How would you like to get rid of the flame on your ass, son?" Watch Your language, God! Still, in exultation I nod so violently, that the flame moves up, tickling my neck. "Ouch!" I scream, "Yes, yes, anything!"

"Good!" quoth You. "If you take my children out of Egypt, I'll douse your fire."

"Oh, no! You really don't want ME!" I protest. "Look, even my parents didn't want me. They took one look at me after I was born, and sent me floating down the Nile in the first reed basket they could lay their hands on. Not a decent naval transport. Can you imagine the trauma of this wet abandonment?" I painfully distort my face. "I'm sure that my stutter is the result of a revived memory...Ouch! What are you doing, Lord?"

The flame has formed a necklace around my neck, and I may at any minute be mistaken for the Fire Eater at Queen Nafartiti's Fertility Carnival. I gyrate violently to evade swallowing the flames—an art that no Hebrew has ever mastered, which gave rise to the ridiculous rumor that I'm an Egyptian Prince pretending to be a miserable Hebrew. I've never heard more ridiculous gossip!

Anyhow, even You, Lord, misunderstood my jerky movements for a nod of agreement. Suddenly I found myself fire-free, a cool breeze caressing my tush, while my lungs fill with fresh air. My mind delights with the stillness of the desert...

Without warning, You, Lord, act like the crazy character in Alfred Hitchcok's "Strangers on a Train," who killed a fellow passenger's wife; then demanded that the widower kill his father as a quid pro quo. I hate to think that my Exodus may end up with a Hitchcokian finale. But this is what I'm hearing: "Now, Moses, I kept my end of the bargain and cleared your tush. Ergo, get your act together and lead my people out of Egypt!"

"What?!"

"What? What?! Don't you know who I am? I am the Lord Thy God, and I don't much care for you having other gods, portable or not. I'm easy to get along with, although I don't want you to think that the Burning Tush is my best trick. I have a vast repertory..."

"But Joseph..."

"Joseph! Joseph! It's time you Egyptian Jews get a life beyond Joseph. Trust me, he was a Dreamer and unreliable. Now, instead of standing around waiting for the Second Coming of Joseph, run along and lead my people out of Egypt."

"But, Lord, I'm too soft-hearted. I couldn't bring even one plague on Egypt, let alone the ten disgusting events You're planning."

"Not to worry. I already took care of this unpleasantness. Even bagged Pharaoh's firstborn for you. From now on it's straight shooting. If you look over yonder horizon, Moses, you'll see My People, from this moment on to be known as your people."

I look towards where the Lord is pointing, figuratively speaking, of course—to where the Red Sea used to be, but no longer is—and there, at a distance, but advancing fast, is a cast of thousands, complete with bleating sheep, cackling chickens and mutinous camels.

"This here is your Hebrew nation," sayeth the Lord, "to be known from here on in as The Multitude."

"Oh, my God!" I stammer with difficulty.

"Why, thank you, Moses."

"But what shall I feed them in the wilderness? A sand cocktail?"

"Not to worry, God will provide."

"That's what you once promised to Onan."

"No, really, I've been working on a new recipe called Manna. It's still half-baked, so to speak, but I assure you that it has my stamp of genius on it."

"How about taste?"

"I don't have that worked out yet. But it looks great…Though it's a tasteless, odorless, colorless…compound…an exalted food of the future."

"When the Multitude is hungry it won't be satisfied with a tasteless, odorless, colorless…"

The Lord cackles. "It's not as bad as you think. The secret is mind over matter. For example: Give them Manna, but instruct them to think brisket, chopped liver, caviar…"

"What's caviar?"

"Never mind. It's too upscale for The Multitude."

"Lord, would You enlighten me: Is the Manna just another trick, like my Burning Tush and the Disappearing Red Sea?"

"Oh, no, it's a miracle. The difference between a trick and a miracle is faith. If you have faith, even Manna can pass for a miracle."

"Very good, Lord." I don't feel like standing in the middle of the desert, with The Multitude on my heels, arguing with God about semantics. As a matter of fact, The Multitude is so close now that right in front, in the first like of attack, her arms gleefully outstretched like a Dragon on opium, is Zippora, my wife of a quarter century.

Since God is unrelenting, I must get as much info upfront as possible. I proceed: "So The Multitude eats Manna and walks in the desert. What's next?"

"Hm, I haven't thought that far ahead. Maybe you have a solution, Moses? You're the one advertising your subdivisions on every camel hyde: 'Moses' Real Estate! We match people to land!'"

He's got me there! I can't think of any plot currently on the market where I can settle The Multitude.

The Lord, again. "How about the land you recently bought from Raman of Ur? I think it starts with C?"

"C...C...C..." Oh, Lord, it's real, I can't talk, You've turned me into a genuine stutterer!!!

"Canaan," He obliges. "Why don't you settle The Multitude in Canaan?"

"I've never even seen the place," I protest. "I don't know the exact location. I got it dirt cheap as backwoods property. No one was bidding on it."

"Sounds like the right place for The Multitude."

"Not at the moment, Lord. I have no deed on me. No papyri. Everything's back home in Goshen."

"Oh, no, Moses. With Me you don't need a deed! You see, I am the Ultimate Settlor. So I give you this land in perpetuity and forever. Be my guests, you and Yonder Multitude."

"Have You ever heard the one about the Hebrew and the Cow?"

"Moses, I'll listen if you promise not to stutter. Genuine or not, it's really annoying."

"I'll try, Lord." With that he freezes the advancing Multitude in place. "Anyhow," I continue, "this old Hebrew, Yankel, has an ancient cow that's also lame, gives no milk, and eats like a vulture. No wonder Yankel decides to sell her. He takes her to the marketplace in downtown Goshen and proclaims in a loud voice. 'Gather around me, oh, ye Children of Israel. Buy my deranged, ungrateful cow that gives no milk and eats like a flock of locust.' Clearly, no one is willing to buy such a cow. Yankel's friend, Mendl, saunters over and says, 'This is no way to sell a cow. Listen to my sales pitch. Gather around, you Children of Jacob and behold this magnificent bovine specimen. Her youthful skin shines in the morning sun, health radiates from every pore in her body. I don't have enough pails to gather all the milk she gives.' Naturally, the bids come fast and furious. Seeing this, Yankel tugs at Mendel's sleeve. 'If she's so good, I'll keep her…'"

"So?" The Lord clears His throat. "Is there a moral in all your ramblings?"

As I think of a reply, I look behind me and see that He has reinvigorated The Multitude. They're getting closer. Closer. Soon they'll be all over me, hugging me, claiming me as their leader. Doesn't He know that I hate to be touched? As everything else in my life, this harkens back to my childhood journey down the river, where I was repeatedly licked by frogs and an occasional domesticated reptile.

"Lord," I say in desperation. "The moral of my story is that I must have a look at this Land of Canaan before I agree to go there…"

"Moses, you have the worst literary transitions…But, very well."

In a second I find myself on a mountaintop overlooking a desolate, hilly landscape of jagged rocks and poison ivy; so different from Egypt's green and pleasant land!

"Oh, no!" I object. "Is this CCCCC?"

"Yeah, it's Canaan! Ain't she grand?" the Lord asks cheerfully.

"How about that plot to the right?"

"Spoken for."

"But it smells like a clogged sewer. Whom do You hate more than The Multitude that You'd want to settle in that filth?"

"Arabs. You see, your cousin Ishmael, who, as you know, was born on the wrong side of the bedsheets, doesn't mind if he wallows in oil."

"So this is Ishmael's reward for Abraham's…Abraham's…"

"Fornicating?"

"Well, indiscretion…with the maidservant Hagar."

It doesn't seem right. "Lord, every tribe elder does this sort of thing. You didn't punish Abraham for running around when he was a Chaldean. But as soon as he becomes a Jew, and sleeps with his first shiksa, whammo…"

"Don't get yourself all worked up, Moses, you're foaming at the mouth."

"Lord, there's a long-standing principle in Egypt's real estate codex: valuable land should not be payment for sexual pecadilloes. A copper necklace, a dozen goats—but not the Arabian Peninsula!"

The Lord chuckles. "You have a point. So, I'll make you a worthwhile swap. Since you have shown how fond you are of cows, instead of oil, I'll give you milk and honey."

"What would The Multitude do with milk and honey?"

"Bake little honey cakes, stupid, to sweeten their lives after all the oppression they suffered in Egypt. And wash it down with jugs of grade AA milk. I have another idea…I'll change the name of the land from Canaan to something more poetic, like the Promised Land?"

"Promised? You mean there's a prior deed…?"

A slight pause. "Well, not actually." I know that whenever someone says "actually," they're about to tell you a lie.

"Who is it, Lord?" I insist.

"Well, the Hivites, but they became the sorry victims of a botched mass circumcision by Jacob's klutzy sons."

"And since then?"

"No one in particular. Trust me."

I am not reassured and peer into the foggy bottom of the Promised Land. And sure enough, it's teeming with creatures scurrying between the rocks. Upon further inspection I identify them as people.

"And who are they?" I inquire.

"Oh, them." Again a pause. "Only the Hittites."

"I thought you said…"

"These are Hittites, with a t, cousins of the Hivites. They're the uncircumcized…"

"But they look alive."

"Oh, don't worry. The Lord doesn't listen to the prayers of the Hittites."

"Lord, I don't like it one bit! I want you to cancel the entire Exodus."

"Too late! The cameras are rolling! It's shaping up as the biggest story since that Baby Pharaoh obscunded with all the palace treasures. No can do, Moses, the whole world is watching!"

I look behind me, and where the Red Sea WAS NOT before—it IS AGAIN. Raging waves, a second Flood! "Oh, my burning…" I groan.

"I know, I know."

At this moment The Multitude gains on me. My wife, Zippora, is hugging me so hard that I break out in hives all over my body. There's time for one more question. "Lord, how long will this Exodus of Yours last?"

But there's no answer. It appears that I've used up all my time.

7

Samson and Delilah
or:
A Lament for the Barbers of Dan

Judges, Chapters 13–16

I am Ketubah, wife of Manoah of the Tribe of Dan, mother of Samson. So why doesn't the Book of Judges refer to me by name, only as "that woman?"

In truth, I'm more interested in the word "naches" than in my own name. Naches is that special glow of satisfaction a parent gets from a child's achievements. Me and Manoah, and our entire tribal Council of Dan, get plenty of naches from my little Samson.

Imagine: My son the Judge!

The road hasn't always been smooth: First, his birth. Although I had been married for a decade, and Manoah came to me every night so we could copulate dutifully, if not always joyfully, to fulfill God's commandment to be fruitful and to multiply. Nada, I was not becoming pregnant. Finally God revealed that He had a secret plan for us, and when God has a plan, you can become an obstetrical success even after a lifetime of barrenness.

Here's how it had gone down: "Woman," sayeth the Lord, jabbing His finger at me, "I'll give you a child. But you'll have to pay the highest price that a mother can pay."

"Like what?"

"Pledge to me that the kid never gets a haircut!"

"Oh, my God!"

"Yes, yes, take your time. Think…"

"But why, Lord, why such extreme harshness?"

"It's not for you to ponder. The Lord works in mysterious ways."

"Meaning, You have no idea why?"

"Yep."

"But otherwise, will he be healthy?"

"Oh, he'll be healthy. Very healthy."

Nine months later I bore my little baby, Samson, who, in fact, resembled a miniature Leviathan.

He was smart enough, I think; but he didn't apply himself to learning, so preoccupied was he with his magnificent mane. Every day he washed it out by the brook, like a girl, conditioning it with honey and goat milk and combing it out with myrtle twigs…My Samson boasted that he could do anything he wanted with his hair. Whenever he would step into the bushes to make love to a fair Hebrew lass, it was with a strict admonition that she dare not stroke his tresses. "I just had my hair done!" he would explain.

Sappar, head of the Barbers' Union of Dan, stalked me everywhere: "Ketubah," he moaned. "Let me give your kid a proper haircut. He'll look mahvellous."

How could I tell him that I've been staying out of his shop on God's order? As a result I spent an awful lot of time at home to avoid running into Sappar and his gang of razor-happy cutters.

Even at his bar-mitsvah, instead of reading the Torah, Samsele fussed with his hair. The fingers that should have held the pointer, were busily combing his silky hair and when he tossed his hair around, it knocked the Torah off the stand and hit the rabbi in the face, blinding him temporarily. The poor guy went "ouch!" the congregation swayed, "Oh, my God;" my darling husband and I were mortified...But Samson the Hero saved the day. "Forget the Haftorah!" he shouted. "Let's eat, drink and be merry!" (Have I forgotten to tell him that together with the admonition of no haircuts, God also said: no booze?)

It did not appear to me that God's plan—whatever it might have been—was working out too well. Perhaps by now He has lost interest in us. After all, there's a limit as to how many jokes you can make about hair!

"The boy must get a haircut!" I told Manoah.

And he responded with his usual: "Yes, dear."

Dawn found us, Samson, and Sappar the Barber, on the tribal mountaintop. It would be a clear, pretty day. A sliver of orange already shimmered beyond the dark hills of Jerusalem. As Sappar lifted his shears, the mountain trembled with God's anger. "Cease and desist!" shouted The Voice. "This boy must hang on to his hair, because I've pledged to transform him into a hermit!"

"Apples and oranges..." started Sappar.

"What?" Apparently God did not understand agricultural metaphors.

"You mean you won't allow him to touch a woman?" the barber was obviously ahead of us.

"No, stupid! That's not what a hermit means!" God laughed good-naturedly. "Au contraire. The holier the hermit, the more women he beds. That's the Jewish way. But, I'll do him one better. Because of his holiness, I shall arrange for him to sleep with Philistine shiksas who fully appreciate a hairy man."

Manoah and I looked at each other pitifully. The Lord cackled. "Besides, parents have little say in the matter."

Is this story getting boring? God apparently thinks so, because at this point he introduces a horrific villain—the Philistines—to liven up the narrative.

At this point in the story my Samson goes down to Timna, in the land of the Philistines, and is smitten by one of their girls. Moreover, he falls in love with her. Quick as a deer, he gallops to his father and me, gushing: "I just met the girl of my dreams! I love her! Oh, yes I do!"

Manoah tries to talk him out of it. "Son, you never really tried to relate to a Jewish girl on an intimate, emotional level."

"Oh, I don't care! This is the woman for me. I want to marry her."

"Hasn't anyone told you that you sleep with shiksas, but do not marry them?"

But, long-haired men are as stubborn as mules. "No, no! I must have this one!" My giant baby stomps his foot, and the primitive tent collapses around us.

It is hard to describe how humiliating it is for low-class Hebrew parents to go bride-hunting to the Philistine Marketplace. Also—as if we need an "also?"—it turns out that the girl Samson picked, is the Ruler's daughter. These uncircumcised want to kill us, drive us into the sea—to which, as yet, we have no access—and we say, just a minute, first, may our son, please, marry your daughter, after which—can you find it in your hearts to kill your new in-laws? So, in conclusion, dear Philistine Ruler, how would you like to climb the mountain next week to have Shabbat dinner with us?"

What I'm recounting here is what was going through our minds while trudging with Samson through the fields of Dan to the Philistine encampment. The idol worshippers, however, have their own bizarre customs: They dispatched a lion to greet us. I swear, one shaggier-looking and more overgrown than my boychik. His appearance should have given us a clue that the Philistine would not be too amenable to my son's proposal. But we, God's Chosen and Gullible, suspected nothing.

Samson, though, has an advantage. God has forewarned him. When the lion bares his teeth and roars at us, Manoah whispers in my ear: "He's up to no good."

"Run, son, run!" we urge our boy. Instead, he places both hands on the lion's gaping mouth—and tears the monster in half. The current score: Jews—1; Lions—0.

The lions swore vengeance.

Samson kicks the lion's carcass onto the side of the road, shakes the cobwebs out of his hair, and marches on to the Philistine girl's house. Her father, hearing of the lion's fate, agrees to the marriage, and takes a raincheck on the idea of putting my son in chains.

Having heard of Samson's fun-loving nature, thirty young Philistines volunteer as his drinking companions and offer to throw him a classy bachelor party. I'm coming up in the world, muses a happy Samson, on the way to the revelry-tent. At that moment he feels an irresistible urge to revisit the lion's cadaver. A ritual designed to say goodbye to his roguish past, I guess.

As he reaches the lion's remains—he sees bees cavorting up and down the dry bones. Brilliantly, he deduces that there's a beehive inside. A curious development, Samson muses, remembering how God promised Moses to give him a land of Milk and Honey. Now half the biblical prophecy resides in a lion's carcass. But, what the hell, honey is sweet, no matter what its receptacle. So he gorges himself all he can, then gathers sprawling leaves to bring the leftovers home to his mother. Later, smacking his lips and sticky with honey, he makes his way to the bachelor party.

The honey-adventure proves to be the party's entertainment. "I'll make you a riddle," says my son. "If you solve it by the end of the seven days of my wedding feast—in the Bible what doesn't come in three's, escalates into sevens—I shall give all thirty of you a roll-up camping blanket and a loincloth with an amorous aphrodisiac sewn into it. But if you fail to come up with the answer, each of you shall give me his blanket and loincloth."

The guests are outraged. "Why should we run around cold and bare-assed while the Hebrew sleeps on thirty blankets and derives potency from 30 loincloths?"

"He who composes the riddles, creates the rules," Samson informs. "So here it is: 'Out of the eater, came forth food/ And out of the strong came forth sweetness.'"

You could have knocked them over with a grape! They stood there, perplexed, for six days and nights. On the seventh, these new so-called "friends," went to Samson's young wife and said: "Either you seduce your husband and tell us the answer to the riddle, or we'll burn down your house and kill your father's lion."

"He's already dead."

"Your Dad?"

"No, the lion. We also found his carcass in the field, but couldn't get close because bees were all over it, so we figured that bees must have built a hive inside and it was filled with honey."

"The honey in the lion has nothing to do with it. Your assignment is to get us an answer to the riddle."

Dealing with her husband, Samson's young wife adopted the Lysistrata method—"No riddle-answers—no sex!"

"No sex?" Samson asked incredulously, staggering on his feet. "Why, that's preposterous! Unthinkable!"

In the next thirty seconds he revealed to her the riddle of the beehive in the lion's belly, and the lady transmitted the message to the thugs.

Samson's ego was savaged, but more importantly, he must find a way to pay his debt. What can a poor Hebrew lad do? The answer is clear: go down to one of the rich Philistine cities—in this case Ashkelon—kill 30 Philistine men and appropriate their blankets and loincloths? After all, a debt is a matter of honor.

Samson's wife was pissed because of the death of so many Philistines. So be it, Samson said peevishly, and returned to Mom and Dad. Ninety days later, still suffering from a case of low self-esteem but needing sex more than pride, he returned to the Valley of the Philistines and demanded that his wife gratify his desires.

"Oh, holy Dagon!" shouted the old Philistine father, as Samson cast a giant shadow on his doorstep. "Hear me out. I gave your wife to another man. Didn't think you'd be back, it's an honest mistake, ha, ha, ha! But, here you are! So please, help yourself to my other virginal daughter."

The man must have learned parenting skills from Lot of Sodom.

"No substitutions!" Samson yelled. "I've had it with your Philistine treachery. If I can't have sex, I'll get the next best thing—violence!"

The Godfather movies couldn't have devised the trick my son came up with. Jewish ingenuity! He went out into the woods and caught himself 300 foxes. Three hundred! What a fashion atatement!

Samson tied each pair of foxes by their tails and placed a flaming torch up their asses. Please don't tell me that God made him do THAT! God is a Deity, not an avenging proctologist! As Samson yelled, "Go foxies, go!" the 300 foxes, with one hundred and fifty burning torches up their asses, stampeded in a panic through every Philistine corn and wheat field, sagely passing over Hebrew fields, just as the Angel of Death had passed over Hebrew homes in Egypt.

(Note to animal activists: The foxes burned!)

The Philistines reacted calmly: They killed Samson's wife and father-in-law, and burned down their house.

Now my prodigal son, Samson, returned to the tribe of Dan and assured everyone that he had sworn off Philistine women for all eternity.

Philistine men, however, continued to chase him. One morning, a multitude of them climbed the hill and confronted Samson at the opening of a cave. Possessing no weapon, Samson was desperate. As his eyes darted over the barren terrain, he saw a donkey's carcass—can you explain to me why he's so attracted to dead animals?—He tore off its bony jaw and taunted the Philistines to come and get him.

Dutifully they approached, one by one, and got clobbered over their heads with a donkey's jaw. 1000 of them! Yes, these are three zeroes! Victory transformed Samson into history's first rapper. Here's the famous ditty: "With the jaw of an ass/ Or a couple of asses/ With the jaw of an ass/ I smote a thousand men."

"I stand before you reborn!" Samson declares to the Children of Israel. "Behold the new, improved Samson! Clean, Jewish, repentant! From here on in I shall devote all my energies to judging you, my people!"

And indeed he did. At least, during the day. But at night he clandestinely roamed through the Red Light District of Gaza, another Philistine city, looking for prostitutes. Shortly, the enemy's Death Squads observed his modus operandi, and staked out an ambush while he was in a seedy motel with a Lady of Ill Repute. It is important to observe that Samson, a man of honor, has never spent an entire night with a slut. He always woke up while darkness reigned outside and hurried home to his Mother.

Soon, however, he found out that the perfidious Philistines had locked the city gates. "Pish, pish," he muttered, retreated a hundred paces, then rammed the gate with his head. It fell. The gate did. All Samson got was a concussion, because he walked away with the city's door-frame on his back. He had no use for it, because we in Israel don't have even one gated city!

The last image that many stunned Gazans retained in their heads was their city gate disappearing, of its own accord, beyond the slopes of Mount Hebron.

Now, one would think that Samson had his fill of non-Jewish girls. Wrong again! But he did learn something: From now on, he said, I'm not marrying them. On the other hand, I'm too old for one-night stands. What I seek is a meaningful relationship with a woman, a lasting commitment, a bonding of kindred souls…And bodies, naturally. Samson without sex is like orange juice without citrus.

But Samson was not the only one to soak up life's wisdom. Even the Philistines grew some brain stems. After dealing with Samson for 20 years they tell themselves: There's got to be something about him that we haven't figured out yet, a secret to explain his unorthodox personal habits, such as his need to mutilate both livestock and beasts...

Shortly thereafter Samson establishes his coveted relationship with a beautiful Philistine lady, what we call in Yiddish "une fille sans profession," known as Delilah. After a while the young woman is visited by all the Philistine lords, who say: "If you find out the secret of Samson's strength, we'll give you 1100—the stakes keep getting higher!—pieces of silver—each!"

Delilah offers Samson a fair exchange: Sex for information. Samson responds by supplying her with misinformation. This, however, is not a victory because the more false data he provides, the less sex he receives. The quality deteriorates as well. Finally, a whole day passes and my son receives but one Lewinsky. Delilah warns that if he doesn't start telling her the truth, all activity below his waist will cease abruptly.

What should a Jewish boy do? God or intercourse? If you don't know the answer, you've never been privy to the thoughts of pious Jewish men during Yom Kippur prayers.

The Good Book puts it this way: Delilah annoyed him so that he had two choices left: Die, or tell her the truth?

Really? Who prevented him from walking out of that door with a friendly SHALOM?

The truth is, Samson wanted so badly to, to...well, you know, that he said the first thing that came to his head: "It's my hair, darling! Because, you see, I'm a monk."

"Oh, sure, and I'm the Virgin Spring!"

The truth is, that Delilah herself was sick and tired of the proceedings and, as stupid as Samson's answer appeared, decided to accept HAIR as the source of his prowess. She transmitted the information via a mail pigeon to the Philistine lords, who rushed to cover her floor with silver pieces.

That night Delilah slipped Samson a Mickey and shaved off his gorgeous tresses. In the morning, the Philistines burst into the tent, attacking a freshly-bald Samson. As he was led away blind and in chains, he cried out in anguish: "I didn't even get laid!"

The perverse Philistines brought Samson, now eyeless, to Gaza—now gateless. They threw him into the dungeon and forced him to turn the grinding wheel, a tedious, unchallenging activity, which, unbeknownst to them, hastened his hair growth.

One day Philistines from all five cities held a reunion in Gaza, in the temple of their chief god, Dagon, who is half man and half fish, but no one knows which half is where. For their religious rites, they gathered crates of rotten tomatoes and placed Samson in between the temple pillars to make it easier for them to pelt him.

So here he stands, covered from head to toe with red juice. Of course, he's desperate. Either do something, he thinks, or die of acid reflux. While he's mulling this over, he experiences an excruciating attack of gastric pain. In order not to fall, he leans heavily against the temple pillars.

Have I told you that in the meantime his hair has grown?

Also, the point against which my son is leaning, is the exact, precise, pin-pointed center of the entire structure. In fact, if a child or a midget leaned on this epicenter— he would have also brought down the temple.

What I'm revealing here for the first time ever is that Dagon's Temple was blown up by gas. The Bible had to provide my son with meaningful last words, and settled for: "Let my soul die with the Philistines?"

In conclusion, the Good Book also says that Samson judged Israel for 20 years. When on earth did he find the time?

8

Moonlighting
or:
Who Killed Uriah the Hittite?

Samuel I, Chapter 16 till end

Samuel II, The Book

Officially I'm Nathan the Prophet. But I also moonlight as Nathaniel the Private Eye, because you can't make a living in Israel as a Prophet. Only the Lord and I are aware of the pros and cons of my Split Personality: As a Prophet I possess divine powers to guess the truth—the reason people hire me as a Private Eye—but when I serve in that capacity, God removes these powers. Please don't tell anyone, my livelihood depends on it. As another member of my profession, Jesus of Nazareth, put it: when I foresee the future, they don't want it; and when they hire me to foresee the future, I'm blind!

How am I doing presently, working two jobs? Comme ci, comme ca, as some of my best friends, the Canaanites, would say. Most days I subsist on dates and wheat cakes—which is great for the digestion!—and lodge in a run-down garret over Jerusalem's wall. I buy a chicken for the Sabbath only on leap year, and always wear the same shabby, but clean, robe.

Enough said about economics.

Moreover, I'm not on good terms with the truth, because in both my professions, people do not want to hear it. As a Prophet—they're ready to stone me; and, as a detective—they demand vindication of their crimes and transgressions. This explains why Nathaniel Investigation, Inc, can hardly afford their sole employee—me!

I am 38 years old, which here, in the tribe of Judah, is considered a young man. Not so with a woman, who, by then, is definitely an old bag. In any event, so far I have muddled through life attracting little fame or prosperity in either profession.

Until that fateful evening in the month of Tammuz when SHE appears at my office door; the rich musk of her jasmine perfume causing my parrot, Moses, to sing the Prelude to the Song of Songs. Personally, I'm not indifferent to the sight of her shapely gams peeking through the folds of her sensuous hand-woven white caftan.

A classy dame, to be sure. Whoever cradles her in his arms, better protect his flank from an attack from the rear.

My nocturnal visitor—did I say it's night?—pulls down her hood, revealing a mass of deliciously cascading russet locks. She leans so close to me that I can smell her sweet breath and taste her delicious spittle.

"This assignment requires the utmost discretion," she cooes like a suckling baby-goat. I nod, unable to speak for fear of betraying the tightness in my—well, whatever.

Something must be said to prove my intelligence. "Aha," I mutter.

"My brother is missing," she whispers in a single breath, as if afraid that if she paused, she'd run out of courage to finish the sentence.

"Aha!"

"Exactly."

I hit myself on the cheek, to awaken from the pleasant reverie of what may happen if I play my cards right.

"Is there something in your eye?" she asks, gazing at my chin.

"Ahem," I choke, overcome with emotion. Quickly I grab my slate and ask, "Your brother, that would be?"

"Uriah." She closes her eyes and opens her mouth wide at the sound of "U." "They call him the Hittite?"

"Why the xenophobic nickname?"

"Because he's a Hittite."

"Ah!" After a pregnant pause, I inquire, "And you?"

"That's for me to know and for you to find out," she giggles flirtatiously.

I clear my throat. "About your brother, then. Can you tell me why you think that he's missing?"

"Because he can't be found."

"Good point." To show off my dexterity, I fiddle with my writing pointer. It falls and, when I jump to pick it up, I lose my balance and crash at her feet. Like an Amorite wrestler, she picks me off the floor and places me back in my chair. Our hands touch, sending a current through our respective bodies. The atmosphere is so thick you can pierce it with a slingshot. To diffuse the awkwardness, we settle back in our seats.

The little lady is way ahead of me. "So," she starts confidently, "three days ago my brother Uriah left the house…"

"Did he go alone?" I interrupt.

"No, with his mule, Barak."

"Any distinguishing marks on the mule?"

"No, just your ordinary Canaanite burro, but one endowed with an agreeable disposition."

"And would you say that the mule has formed an unnatural attachment to your brother?"

"Let's talk about Uriah."

"If you say so," I agree peevishly, making it clear that she should let me be the judge of what's relevant and what isn't.

She bites her pretty lip. "The troubling part is that I don't think my brother's marriage is working out too well…"

"He's married, then?"

"Why, yes?"

"Because, young lady, for all we know, this may have some relevance to the case. Perhaps as much as the mule. And to what name, does she, the wife, answer to?"

"Bat Sheva."

"Oh, you mean, Bat Sheva who's married to Uriah the Hittite, King David's general?"

"Why, yes."

"I knew it!" I happily slap my thigh with my writing tablet, which hurts so much I have to massage myself gently. "I am sure that these two, Bat Sheva and Uriah, will go down in history linked together like Romeo and Juliet..."

"But I told you it's not working out."

"Hasn't worked out for Romeo and Juliet either. But if you insist, I shall make a note: No loving bond..."

"Bond? You mean, James Bond? Do you think I should have hired him?"

"Don't even think of it! His name in Hebrew is Oy Oy Sheva, and that alone would mess up our investigation."

"Then, I guess, it's my beshert-karma," agrees my beauteous apparition. In sudden anger, she bangs her fist on my table. The potshards rattle ominously. "I think that my sister-in-law, Bat Sheva, did him in. You see, he left the house briefly to fetch a goatskin of milk, and never returned, as if the earth swallowed him up."

"Maybe it did," I offer. "Like the sons of Korach."

"No! That was an uncivilized time, when the Jews wandered in the desert. Also, the earth has a habit of swallowing the Children of Israel, not Hittites."

She gets up brusquely. I admire her, she's one dame with a natural streak of resolve. "By the way," she says. "My name is Moriah, sister of Uriah, daughter of Tekiah of Pekiah."

I am making furious notes. Before I can say: Holy Tseruiah! she drops a bag of silver shekels in my lap and vanishes into the night.

The first breakthrough in the investigation occurs when an anonymous tip arrives in my office from Shayna, custodienne of the Turkish Bath, to the effect that the aforementioned Bat Sheva, sister-in-law of Moriah, has been seen taking a bath with one David, son of Jesse of Bethlehem…"

The name sounds vaguely familiar. Who can the rascal be? I go out to speak to my new secretary Dahlia, daughter of Dliath. (Moriah's money made the expansion of my office and staff possible.) "Dahlia, you know everyone in Jerusalem. Does the name David Son of Jesse, ring a bell?"

"Let me think," she broods, "David, David?" I like that gal. A no-nonsense, savvy broad, fast on the uptake and no histrionics. Doesn't mind milking my goat, either, if you get my drift?

For a week I question Jerusalemites from all walks of life and peel off the first layer of truth: Said David, Son of Jesse, is none other than King David. Five more days of legwork yield his address: King David's Palace, on the Tower of David, in the City of David.

Finally, a solid break in the case!

Suddenly the investigation takes on a more sinister thrust: Have David and Bat Sheva been bathing in the nude? In other words, was His Majesty in the altogether, but altogether, and altogether...?

I don't remember the rest of the lyrics.

I am speaking to you now in my other personality: asNathan the Prophet. It behooves here to disclose a few facts about our King. For example: his propaganda machine has created an exaggerated warrior myth around a minor youthful encounter with an overgrown Philistine hooligan named Goliath. Jewish boys have had these fights for hundreds of years. It's a rite of passage, a natural part of growing up. But when our David successfully threw a pebble into the center of the Philistine's forehead, he grabbed the harp and began to sing his own praises. The Jews, a musically-endowed race, were so impressed that they elected him King.

Even God was surprised. "Nathan," he asked me, "how did the shrimp do it?"

Well, I explained , it's always easy to pick a fight with someone bigger than yourself. And this Goliath was huge, gigantic...But, unlike David's later spin, he was not as huge as Masada or the fortified city of Jericho.

Let me recapitulate the essential facts of the event: Old King Saul's army was camped out in the Wadi, opposite multitudes of Philistines from five cities. Young David looked around and said: What a waste! You see, he had a secret weapon: Red Hair! What does red hair have to do with slaying Goliath? Plenty! A freckled redhead has no business gallivanting in the midday sun, and most especially not to put on a coat of arms on his itching, peeling body. Which is the reason why David wore a white cloak and used five small pebbles, instead of a heavy burning sword. Actually he was aiming at Goliath's unprotected heel, when he hit the tiny brain stem in the center of his cranium.

Gazing at Goliath who lay at his feet, David said: Shucks, I need a souvenir. He tried to lift the Philistine's helmet, but it was too heavy, so he chopped off the entire head and walked away dragging it behind him.

When King Saul beheld the headless body, he screamed: "Where's the head? By droit de seigneur—I want the head!"

The King sent emissaries to David and demanded that he surrender the head. David greeted the King, holding up the head by its long black hair, when along came the King's beautiful son, Jonathan. David was so beguiled by the lad, that he dropped the disputed head and followed Jonathan, open-mouthed.

So the King had the head and David had the son.

Saul said, "David, the last thing we need is a gay scandal among the People of the Book. So take my daughter's hand. Now you have the hand, and I have the head."

Lord, I think that we have too many body parts in this story.

You may ask, which of Saul's children did David love more: Jonathan or Mihal? The answer is: Both! As everyone knows, Hebrew redheads are sexually voracious. He had women, he had men, and one may wonder about all the nights of his youth that he'd spent with the sheep. What greatly enhanced his sexual prowess—no, it's not what you think!—was his music. Yes, our lad from Bethlehem was a poet, a singer, and a lute player. Day and night he serenaded the lovely lasses—and laddies—of Israel, and they serenaded him in return.

It was driving King Saul bonkers.

To soothe the King's madness David provided him with other people's body parts: Philistine foreskins, because Saul was disenchanted with Goliath's head, which had already shriveled beyond recognition. At this juncture the merry men of Judah learned another diplomatic truth: It is easier to separate a dead Philistine from his foreskin than a live one.

Whatever you may think about David, he is the first Jewish workaholic: Carries on loving, simultaneous, affairs with Jonathan and Mihal; fights the Philistines on Mondays and Thursdays; escapes from King Saul's murderous rages on Sundays and Tuesdays; and, in between, plays the harp and composes the Book of Psalms.

The Good Book says that after David became King he conquered Jerusalem, scaling a high hill and defeating the mighty Jebusite army. Not true! Or, what the Amalekites call a bold-faced lie! The truth is that all Jews suffer from vertigo, an ingrained fear of heights. So David and his men crawled into the city through the water hole, and, upon entering, discovered that the walls were manned by blind and lame wooden dolls. The Jebusites' message to the Jews: Our city is so mighty, the blind and the lame can protect it.

Incidentally, today there are no more Jebusites.

But all is not well with the Jews, either. You see, as long as David lived in tents, with heads and foreskins, he was a happy man. But once he conquered Jerusalem and built himself a beautiful palace, he spent too much time on the roof, gazing at the stars.

And that's how he saw beautiful, young Bat Sheva. The logistics of roof-climbing baffle me too, but rulers have ingenious ways of picking up young chicks.

This is Nathaniel, the P.I. Where are we?

Oh, yes, who killed Uriah the Hittite?

Isn't it obvious that the Wine Steward did it?!

9

Is P.E. P.C.?
i.e.
Is the Prophet Elijah Politically Correct?

Kings I, Chapter 18

It's not easy to be editor of the Book of Kings in the Bible. My name is Mendele Orech Seforim, the man whose desk sports the famous literary adage: "The shekel stops here." It means that the final authority as to what goes into, or is omitted from, the Book, is mine. I have substituted a clever P.S. to many of the irrelevancies in the Kings' lives, such as: "And the rest of the doings of King Blah Blah Blah are inscribed in the Book of Chronicles…" They don't even have an editor.

My anthology, Kings, is no mere chronicle. Here you not only make a judgement call as to what to include and how much, but also in what manner it should be interpreted. What face do I put on a story so that it remains favorable to the masters I serve, namely the Kings of Judah, for whose benefit every three sentences I repeat some variation of the following statement: King David has always done right in the eyes of the Lord, (except for the minor unpleasantness of ordering the death of Uriah the Hittite).

Some of the inaccuracies I put in the book continue to haunt me. I am a man of integrity, a rare breed in this corrupt generation. As a scrupulous chronicler of the truth, I have always been guided by the highest principles and moral standards. But if this truth is not favorable to the House of David—it must fly out of my tent into the vast desert of oblivion.

Luckily, in the Book of Kings I don't have to tell any direct lies. Not that I always volunteer the truth...In fact, some unkind souls refer to me as slippery ocean slime, the kind that we, Jews, are forbidden to eat.

Candidly, though, as far as matrimony is concerned, King David was a man of moderation, who practiced strict self-discipline and married only 33 wives. With constant battles against the Philistines, and building a kingdom, there was little time left for a poet to devote to romance.

But his son, Solomon, inherited a thriving economy, secure borders, and an ever-mounting tax base. "Ah," he gushed, "I can love all I want."

And love he did!

1000 wives! That's three zeroes! To Solomon the earth was the limit, as he imported wives from Algiers to Zanzibar, a veritable Rainbow Coalition. And, with no more than a dozen exceptions—loved them dearly and aimed to please.

King Solomon's reign was a nightmare of scheduling. He possessed building-plans and diagrams of all the structures in which wives were housed, arrows to the easiest access routes from one bedroom to another, and exact mathematical calculations of time spent in each. Although, he was the first equal-opportunity lover, his amorous movements were strictly planned. The amount of foreplay was rationed, and a barely-justifiable quota of orgasms was allocated per wife. But, even with the best intentions, rumor had it that this husband of 1000 wives, did not always rise to the occasion.

And when Solomon died—in transit, by the way—I describe him in the book as "a very old man." Not strictly true because he was only 50, but had become withered and gaunt from running through long and windy hallways, to meet the expectations of so many sex-starved ladies.

P.S. As an afterthought I looked up Solomon's projected itinerary for the evening of his death: He was en route from the Edomite to the Hittite, while ahead of him were still the Moabite, Ammonite, and Egyptian princesses. May the Lord admit him to a Moslem Paradise!

Even God suffered from a bad case of Solomon Fatigue, and fixed it so that his son, King Rehoboam, was impotent. All the mothers who brought their daughters to the new King's palace, expecting a complete harem turnover, received a strange message: "The King doesn't want your daughters. He wants your money!"

"Oh, no!" the parents said, crestfallen. "The deal is supposed to be that we get the money, and he takes the daughters."

"No!" the courtiers insisted. "You keep the girls, but give us the money!"

The people were so disgusted that they departed, leaving behind neither girls nor money.

Moreover, 10 of the tribes established their own kingdom, and called it Israel. Solomon's son was King of Judah, with residence in Jerusalem. I, Mendele Orech Seforim, am in the employ of the Kings of Judah.

Enough said.

My mission—whether I want to accept it or not—is to prove that everything is bigger and better in Judah than in Israel, which proves yet again that God loves Judah more.

Certain matters, of course, are indisputable. Our capital, Jerusalem, is built on a taller hill than theirs, Samaria. We also have the Temple and all the celebrity Prophets, such as Isaiah, Jeremiah, and my own brother, the Great Prophet Menahem Mendel. In Israel they haven't produced one prophet with a quotable sound-bite.

Until—and here's where my life enters into its dark phase—word comes to us in Jerusalem that the Israelites claim to have a Prophet Du Jour, one Elijah of Gilead, a giant of Mosaic proportions and unforgettable oratory.

My Lord, King Asa of Judah, is as mad as hell. "Greatness in Israel? Impossible! Outrageous! Quick, Mendel Orech, go north and check out what gives with this Elijah." Naturally, even though it's unsaid, I'm expected to prove that Elijah is a dwarf, a pygmy, a stuttering impostor.

I pick up my gnarled wooden staff, keffyah headdress, and white robe—standard issue of Central Casting—and trudge up north to the Hills of Israel.

It is summer and as hot as hades. A drought has befallen the land, not a drop in wadis, nooks, or crannies. Now, I must explain something about this business of droughts: You don't have to be a prophet, or even a soothsayer, to predict a drought. In this land there's always drought. It's hot, the sun scorches our bodies, and the desert sand fills our mouths and lungs...So predicting a drought takes no talent, and God has nothing to do with it. It's the climate, stupid! Not until people figure out how to lay pipes across the desert and irrigate their fields, will we have relief from the drought.

I stop in the first little town I reach. A dozen mules, one horse, black tents, a saloon. As I ask passers-by "Where's Elijah?" they jab their fingers pointing north. But I am bone-weary, so I stop to schmooz people in the saloon and to treat them to a round of their beloved local specialty: Goat milk with honey and arak. Yum yum.

After several rounds their tongues loosen up, and I learn the current local gossip: Their King Ahab is a weakling married to a domineering bitch called Jezebel. So what else is new? For that kind of scoop I didn't have to travel to Israel! It also appears that she's a Lebanese shiksa who has never converted to Judaism, but promised to raise the children Jewish—while knowing all the time that she's barren! Now, that's goyim for you!

I nod my head in sympathy.

But—and here the men's eye light up—she's beautiful, pure knock-your-socks-off gorgeous. Tall and busty like the Coptic goddess of Fertility—even if she's barren!

Her lovely long legs seem to grow right out of her boobs and her feline eyes bespeak of ecstasy.

I nod with appreciation. Last year I spent a week in Beirut and know that there's nothing better than a Lebanese shiksa.

Says an ancient goatherd with rheumy eyes: "It's true that this woman turned our King Ahab into a worshipper of the god Ba'al, that ugly creature who's half man and half frog. Coming to think of it, not that huge a price. Though I personally prefer the Egyptian goddess Astarte, whose luxurious little carvings are a pleasure to caress."

With that the men reach for their figurines of the busty Astarte, and start fondling her breasts. I offer the old goatherder five shekels to have a go at his.

"Go fondle the frog," he replies petulantly.

Ungrateful prodigal!

Their first passion satisfied, the gentlemen put away their idols. Says a young man with slender fingers and a black goatee: "All things being equal, we must forgive Queen Jezebel for slaughtering the Prophets of God."

"Slaughtering the Lord's Prophets?" my ears perk up.

I order another round, and press for details. Alas, they have little information. It seems that the Queen's security police rounded up the men at night, and killed them off secretly. No bodies have been found to allow for prosecution.

"What does Elijah say to this?" I venture.

The old man chuckles. "Elijah is not a happy man." A sparkle appears in his eyes. "You know, you can meet Elijah in person. He's called a general conference of the tribes on Mt. Carmel."

I thank the men. It seems, after all, that the money on drinks has been well spent.

Mt. Carmel is also parched, though its lush trees and vegetation make it look prettier than the desolate hills. Lovely caves dot the mountainside, one called till this day Elijah's Cave, because here our Prophet fortified himself with figs and raisin wine before going out to address the Multitude.

To give you an idea of what Elijah looks like, think of Chuck Heston. All the familiar props: the long white beard, the white robe, Biblical sandals, and the booming voice. "Oh, Children of Israel, we have gathered atop this mountain to discuss ways of bringing forth the rain."

So now it's Elijah the Rainmaker! Very well, if he can do this, I shall personally proclaim him a Prophet—the King of Judah be damned!

"What we'll do today," says Elijah, "is perform an ecumenical prayer service, with members of all religions joining in unified supplication. For that purpose we have gathered here the 450 priests of Ba'al..."

Servants uncover a makeshift leaf structure, under which are hidden 450 young men dressed in little green robes with frogs embroidered over their hearts. The young men grin and take a bow.

"And on this side," Elijah intones in his commanding voice, "are the 400 priests of Astarte." Revealed are 400 equally happy lads, dressed in pink robes, with tits and ass embroidered over their hearts. The T.A.'s bow before the Israelites.

"Children of Israel! You have a clear choice!" Elijah bellows. "Me, or them!" He motions towards the pinks and the greens. The people are silent, dumbfounded. I can tell right off that they don't like what's coming—i.e. a gigantic dose of Jewish guilt.

As if on cue, Elijah's servants bring out two heifers. The fiery Prophet grabs the pretty, red one. "Mine!" he yells. The other, imperfect beast, is turned over to the priests of Ba'al. Graciously Elijah says: "You first."

As agreed, they slaughter the heifer and put the chunks of meat on a pile of dry sticks; but do not ignite it. "Dance before your lord Ba'al, and if he's a real god he'll produce the fire to cook your beef," Elijah cooes.

Clever, ha?

So the priests of Ba'al prance before their raw supper, making a spectacle of themselves to the delight of the Children of Israel. Exactly at noon, Elijah stops the proceedings. "Enough! Now it's my turn!"

Expertly, he slaughters his heifer and throws the meat on a different pile of dry twigs, one that's been directly under the blazing sun, presently in its zenith. Elijah merely takes a two-step to the right and a shimmy to the left. And Hubba Dubba. the sun sparks the twigs and fries Elijah's sacrifice to perfection.

"Ah!" sigh the people.

"Why didn't we think of that?" wonder the priests of Ba'al.

Elijah claims that the fire is a divine indication that God is the real Lord, and Ba'al an idle idol. He produces a recently-sharpened, long knife. Caressing its blade, he purrs in a whisper that reaches the furthest corners of the crowd: "Let's waste the foreign bastards!"

"Oh, no, not us!" the people respond. "We wash our hands from this one."

"You cowards! You old ladies! You, you..." Elijah almost chokes with rage, but the people refuse to follow orders. So Elijah, singlehandedly, butchers all 450 priests of Ba'al.

Must have been a really sharp knife.

And if you think that the 400 pink priests of Astarte returned home that night to have dinner with their mothers—think again!

I return to King Asa and report that in all my travels I failed to meet up with Elijah.

Epilogue

THE NEW TESTAMENT ON THE QUESTION;

IS SEX GOOD FOR THE JEWS?

(Over)

ANSWER:

THE IMMACULATE CONCEPTION

About the Author

Rachel Patron is a journalist who asks the hard questions. She is a frequent contributor to the Hartford Courant and other national newspapers. She has a Bachelor Degree from the Hebrew University in Jerusalem and a Masters in Journalism from U.C.L.A. She and her husband reside in Bloomfield, Connecticut.